THE BATTLES OF SUNUPSVILLE

THE BATTLES OF SUNUPSVILLE

RUFUS CRIS-KARGBO

THE BATTLES OF SUNUPSVILLE

iUniverse books may be ordered through booksellers or by contacting:

iUniverse
1663 Liberty Drive
Bloomington, IN 47403
www.iuniverse.com
1-800-Authors (1-800-288-4677)

ISBN: 978-1-6632-0490-5 (sc)
ISBN: 978-1-6632-0491-2 (e)

Library of Congress Control Number: 2020913001

Print information available on the last page.

iUniverse rev. date: 07/17/2020

CONTENTS

Chapter 1   A Planet of Sun-Powered Fighters 1

Chapter 2   Enemy Infiltration from Another Planet 17

Chapter 3   Sunia and the Army of Zimen 31

Chapter 4   The Rearview Mirror of Plusia's War
             Campaign 53

Chapter 5   The Systematic Takeover of Ousia 69

Chapter 6   Zimen Defend Sunuspville 75

A Planet of Sun-Powered Fighters

We are products of storms, and when others run away from them, we run to them and furnish tables in their very presence.

S unia pushed his chair five feet away from his desk and stretched both of his arms wide, causing his shoulder joints to crackle. Then he leaned backward with his eyes facing the ceiling, rested his head on the headrest of the ergonomic chair, and raised his fountain pen to his mouth. He bit its cap tightly as he gazed at the grey tiles on the ceiling of his study room for about twenty minutes. Suddenly, he heard a little bang on the glass window. It momentarily disrupted his focus and his thought process. He glanced in the direction of the window and saw a gray kingbird and a black raven fighting in midair.

The raven fluttered her wings and took off in the direction of the mangrove tree down the yard; the kingbird chased after her with ferocious speed. The raven landed on a big leafy branch of the mangrove tree; the kingbird landed on the raven and poked her on the neck several times with her short beak causing some leaves to tremble and few feathers to fly off in different directions. The raven responded in kind, sinking her strong beak into the wings of the kingbird provoking a loud, arresting call of distress from the brave kingbird before he flew away into the sunny skies and disappeared out of sight. Thereafter, the raven turned her thick neck to the left and right. She shook her feathers back into place as if shaking off the encounter with the kingbird. She gave out a loud croaking sound, lifted her wings, and flew in the direction of the setting sun.

Sunia shifted his focus to the pictures on his desk. He picked them up one after the other, looked at them thoroughly, and whispered to himself, "There will always be wars until the first people stop preventing others from becoming first, and boundaries are respected." Then he got up, paced back and forth on the floor of his study room several times, walked back to his desk, and arranged the files and papers neatly. Finally, he put on his sneakers, left the house, and went jogging toward the center of the city of Plesorhub.

He jogged north of Sunupsville, climbed up the mountains, and descended into the city of Plesorhub via the only dirt trail that connected the two cities. The route took him through blinding curves and a dense forest of oak trees. He was intentionally avoiding attention along the crowded highways. After jogging fifteen miles at a sustained pace of five miles per hour, he reached Broadway Street. He continued west along this street, his heated body sending steam into the atmosphere as he wiped the sweat off his brow. By the time he got halfway along Broadway Street, it was six minutes past six o'clock in the evening.

About a kilometer down the road from him, six Yumen sat at a round table made of solid mahogany wood outside the Buzia night club. The wine glasses in front of some of them contained Friskey-Six, a specially made wine with a very high level of alcohol. Those who drank it saw everything as shadows. There were beer bottles in front of others. The Yumen were talking and laughing out loud. Soggy, the social leader of the six, spotted Sunia as his three-hundred-five-pound frame bounced off the road due to his long legs. Soggy pointed in the direction of Sunia and said to the others, "Hey! Look! Here comes Sunia!"

"Oh, my gosh! Sunia! It's Sunia. Here comes the tallest and possibly the strongest Yumen in all of Planet Ousia!" said the Yumen who was sitting on Soggy's immediate left. "Wow! Can you believe this guy is eight feet two inches tall? Watch his steps! He surges forward like a locomotive train—a graceful display of strength and power!"

"How tall are you?" Soggy asked the Yumen on his immediate left.

"I am seven foot three," he replied.

"Really? So, you grew three feet taller in the last few seconds to deprive me of six bottles of Friskey-Six wine? Notwithstanding, I am three inches taller than you are, and you are going to buy me three bottles of Friskey-Six wine right now!" This provoked loud laughter from the other four Yumen.

He responded by pointing his bony finger at Soggy and asked, "Based on your logic, how many bottles of wine will you buy for Sunia?"

"Sunia is a teetotaler. He does not drink alcohol," replied Soggy with a grin on his face. "Hey, guys, have you noticed that most Yumen are in the seven-foot range?"

One of the Yumen, who was sitting right across the table from Soggy, was busy gulping Friskey-Six. He dropped his glass on the table and muttered, "Hey, Soggy, do you know how old Sunia is?"

"He must be in his early forties. I'm pretty sure he's forty-four years old. Listen up, guys! Enough talk about numbers. I have an idea," said Soggy.

"What's the idea? I hope you're not thinking of challenging him to a duel, because a great number of Yumen in Ousia think you're strong too," exclaimed the other to his left.

Soggy rubbed his metal chest, stretched both of his arms, and said, "No, no, no! Not today. This is the day to imbibe not bout. Besides, Yumen don't fight each other. Rather, we can pose to him all the questions about the power and relevance of the Sun to the safety and existence of Ousia."

"That is a great idea," said another, and all six of them agreed. When Sunia got to where they were sitting, they waved at him to get his attention and beckoned him to come over and sit down for a short break and a meaningful conversation. At their invitation, Sunia crossed over to the other side of the road to where the six Yumen were sitting and greeted them with a broad smile and warm handshakes. After the exchange of pleasantries, the Yumen offered Sunia a seat, and he sat down. Soggy reached for Sunia's right hand again, with both of his hands shook it warmly and introduced himself. "My name is Soggy, and these are my

Broadway friends. Besides seeing you on television, I haven't seen you in a long time, and didn't expect to see you in this part of town. My gosh! Look at you—you're in great shape!"

"Thanks, Soggy! It is always good to see you; I have not seen you in ages. It's the ideal day to meet an old warrior—when the western sky of Plesorhub is pregnant with dark clouds ready to give birth to a storm. Tell me, how may I help you?"

"Sunia! We are products of storms, and when others run away from them, we run to them and furnish a table in their very presence. Listen, Sunia! What I am about to say is important, and I want you to give me your undivided attention."

Sunia pointed at his ears with both of his index fingers and said, "Right now, I call these ears, Soggy. Speak! I am listening."

"Sunia, whatever I look at after looking at the Sun, I see shadows. The most troubling thing is that my friend on my immediate right thinks that what we call the Sun is a mere figment of our imaginations. According to him, the Sun does not exist even though he felt its heat. Tell me—tell us—son of the Sun, when you look at the Sun, what do you see?"

Sunia knew the social and security implications of the question. He adjusted his buttocks on the seat and steadied his gaze as if to wrap his mind around the question. He knew his answer to this very important question. Because of his reputation, he could help make or break Yumen and define the quality of Ousia's fighting force for generations to come because Yumen would surely quote him. "Your friend who told you the Sun is a figment of the Yumen imagination could be the victim of the Broadway justification rule: it is the propensity to choose selfish pleasure when it conflicts with a civic or moral obligation anchored in reality supported by overwhelming evidence and to justify the choice by dismissing obligation and the fight against reality. However, a fight against reality is a distraction to reality and imprisons purpose. Notwithstanding, fellow Yumen, when I look at the Sun, I see power, I see beauty, I see a purpose, and I see you. But it also makes me fight better," replied Sunia. Wanting to get more clarification, Sunia said to Soggy, "Tell me about the shadows. Do you see shadows of Yumen or do you see Yumen as shadows?"

Soggy planted both of his elbows on the table, opened wide the palms of his hands, and brought both palms together so that they touched each other. Then he slowly dropped his chin into the fork of his hands. Looking right into Sunia's scarlet-colored eyes, he said, "Everything I look at, including Yumen, appears as shadowy, lifeless shadows, and this makes me feel like a shadow too. My frustration was heightened when my doctor told me my eyes are healthy. I hope my doctor's eyes are healthy too and that he used the right instrument to check my eyes." Soggy paused and, with a look of frustration in his eyes, whispered, "My concern deepened when all five of my friends told me they experienced the same thing and this recent phenomenon happens only when they look at the Sun from Broadway Street. Also, we have noticed that most of the Yumen on Broadway Street act like shadows. They are purposeless and powerless. The energy and motivation to remain the fighting force of Ousia is dying slowly." Then he blinked his eyes several times and opened them wide, stretching his eyelids to the very limit.

"Soggy, our fathers told us that, when a man's eyes swell up like yours, it means his body clock has been tampered with. Your head seems to be resting on one of the many forks of life's road. Soggy, when was the last time your brain had a good natural rest?"

"I rest my brain on these bottles of Friskey-Six wine," replied Soggy.

"That rest is unnatural and temporary, and when you wake up tomorrow morning, you will find yourself trapped in the same spot with long chains wrapped around your head. You will be like a lamb pulled down a starless path by an unknown force."

"Sunia, you have painted a very bleak picture of my tomorrow, but I stopped thinking in terms of a tomorrow a long time ago. That is not to deny the reality of a future, but to tame the future."

"Tame the future? Tell me, Soggy, how do you tame the restless unknown?" asked Sunia with a look of surprise written across his face.

"Sunia, I don't know! However, I tame my future by multiplying these bottles." He referred to the bottles of Friskey-Six on the table in front of him. "They are strong enough to put my brain to eternal sleep." Soggy took his hands off the table and leaned back in his chair. He grabbed the top end of his five-inch goatee with his right hand, ran his hand down to the last strand of hair, and then used the same hand to rub both of his eyes as if to wipe the alcohol out of them.

"Soggy, when we put our brains to sleep, we become

mere shadows of Ousia's fighting forces. We also become potent weapons in the hands of foreign forces," said Sunia. Sunia stood up, looked at the other five Yumen one after the other, and asked, "Are you all shadows too?"

All six of them raised their heads, looked straight into Sunia's eyes, and nodded their heads in affirmation. Then Sunia banged on the table with his right hand and shouted, "*No! Never!* The fighting force of Ousia is not a shadow and will *never* be a shadow! We inherited a proud tradition of military dominance from our forebears, and we have to walk in the footsteps of that tradition. I suggest you take a crash course on the war history of Ousia to learn the scale and sweep of her triumphs. Please do yourselves a favor—make a trip to the Museum of War History and read the stories of the impact of her thousands of boots on the necks of her enemies. It was real! It was powerful!"

Soggy dropped his wine glass. All six men dropped their wine glasses on the table one after the other. They leaned forward and listened to the words of Sunia with rapt attention. "Also, I advise you to look at the Sun from location other than Broadway Street and without Friskey-Six in your veins. Try that! Maybe you might have a different experience." Then Sunia stood up. He shook hands with each of them and said, "I have to keep this high adrenalin level going before it wanes, so I have to continue jogging. But remember that on your shoulders, Yumen, rests the security of Ousia. She would not have been able to conquer the scorpions and pythons of history if she had depended on shadows. Adjust your lenses, redeem your purposes, and strive to regain your fighting edge as unbeatable defenders of Ousia!"

After those words, Sunia bade them good-bye and took off jogging. He jogged about sixty feet, stopped, and turned around. With six pairs of eyes fixed on him, he shouted at the top of his lungs as if sending a message to all Yumen: "Remember! It is not a dream! It is not a shadow! The enemies of Ousia are real, and Ousia needs real men to fight her battles!" He turned around again and continued jogging as the buildings echoed his words in the ears of the six Yumen. Before he disappeared out of their sight he shouted again, "Shadows don't win wars! Shadows do not build factories! Yet Ousia's fighting force is turning into shadows!"

But this time Soggy and his friends did not hear him because Sunia was far away, and Soggy and his five friends had turned their attention back to the bottles of Friskey-Six wine in front of them. Then Soggy poured some of it into his glass and into the glasses of the others. He lifted his glass to his lips and took a gulp. As the wine made its way into his stomach, he declared, "With this, I numb my pain and drown all my failures and frustrations in the deep ocean of chemical pleasure." Then he lifted his glass, which was half-full of wine, and tapped it against the glasses of the others. They all whispered, "Cheers to friendship—the Broadway Street friendship!"

Thereafter, Soggy ordered some Plesordol. This was a drug that came in the form of white nickel-sized tablets that, when ingested, gave the user extreme pleasure. But the user also suffered from extreme diplopia and a total loss of touch with reality. Each of them took a tablet and drank more glasses of wine.

Sunia jogged to the end of Broadway Street, turned

around, and jogged back toward his home in Sunupsville. When he got to where the six Yumen were sitting, he noticed the number had increased to eighteen. He slowed down and waved at them, but they did not wave back so he continued jogging. "Maybe they are seeing a shadow and not Sunia," he whispered to himself. "But wait a minute! The other twelve don't look like Ousians! Some of them look just like the guys in the pictures on my desk!" He jogged all the way north of Broadway Street and climbed the mountains of Sunupsville. When he got to the top of the mountain, he did three rounds of forty-four press-ups and lay down in the grass with his eyes facing the Sun. Sunia had stood on that mountain many times before, but this time the beauty of Ousia and the gathering storm of darkness on Broadway Street sought to mar that beauty that occupied his mind. Ousia was an exquisite planet; she had all the trappings of a vacation spot with breathtaking landscapes and crystal-clear rivers dressed in state-of-the-art ocean liners. Her sparkling white-sand beaches, always strewn with half-naked beings basking in the ever-present pleasure of midnight, were the envy of inhabitants of other planets. The Yumen had made all her highways twelve lanes, six lanes on each side, with intricate flyovers that ran close together and then branched out to link scattered communities to massive metropolises. The roads and the architecture of the buildings displayed the sheer genius of Ousia's civil engineers. Roads ran through mountains of rock, mansions were built deep beneath the ground, and hotels were built eighteen feet above the ground, held by invisible pillars, making the hanging garden of Nebuchadnezzar seem a mere toy. Ousia's giant shopping malls, night clubs, exquisite restaurants, dazzling beauty parlors, and massage centers displayed jaw-dropping beauty and earned planet Ousia the nickname Paradise Extraordinaire. The capital city of Ousia was Plesorhub, and the main street that ran from the north side of the city to the south side of the city was Broadway Street.

One hundred and twenty-two million intelligent fighting beings called Yumen inhabited planet Ousia. They looked and functioned just like human beings except their chest and stomach areas consisted of a metal construction known as a Doby. The chest segment of the Doby was a metal weapons holster vest that had two chambers, each loaded with electric flaming swords and a SLAWTAD (sea, land, and air weapons trace destroyer) missile launcher called the Lous. The Lous had metal sliding doors that protected and hid the interior workings from view and operated through signals from the brain. When the brain signaled the Lous to shoot a target with a particular weapon, both metal sliding doors of the Lous would slide open, exposing the selected chamber. The weapon of choice would automatically position itself, and swords or missiles would be released and directed to whatever the Yumen focused his eyes on. Again, when the brain sent another signal for the weapon to stop, the weapon would stop and slide back into its chamber. The metal sliding doors would then shut. This made the Lous and the brain the most powerful parts of the Yumen makeup, but Yumen harnessed their power through what they called the Sun-concentration exercise. To do this exercise, the Yumen would lie flat on their backs with their eyes looking straight at the Sun while their Lous, which had an inbuilt battery to power the metal sliding doors and the weapons systems, like solar cells, sucked up the Sun's energy to provide constant power for its weapons so the Yumen would always be battle ready.

Thus, planet Ousia saw no need for a standing army because every Sun-charged Yumen was a soldier of Ousia and could defend her against any enemy invasion. Unfortunately, some Yumen ignored the Sun-concentration exercises and focused solely on themselves and exploring the long Broadway Street menu of destructive pleasures. This caused them to lose power, which made their weapons inoperable. This, in turn, affected their ability to fight well when they were attacked. Also, the lack of Sun-concentration exercise slowly changed the color of their eyes from a distinctive scarlet to silver, thus affecting the way they viewed and interpreted reality. This was the reason people from other planets referred to planet Ousia as the silver planet.

Notably, Yumen loved wearing hats. For this reason, every Yumen in Ousia wore a golden cone-shaped hat. It was a reminder to engage in the Sun-concentration exercise, with its head pointing to the heavens and its base firmly resting on the head as if to form a boundary against Dobymin and Lousomin chemicals. Ousians believed every Yumen had two door-shaped cells in the head loaded with Dobymin and Lousomin chemicals respectively. These chemicals controlled Yumen and had to be monitored; otherwise, the enemy could use the Yumen as entry points to gain access into the planet. Dobymin was a chemical at the back of the head that supplied pleasure and triggered indulgence; on the other hand, Lousomin was a chemical in the frontal part of the head that fueled self-centeredness.

Experience had shown that planet Ousia functioned well when Yumen maintained control over these two chemicals and channeled them toward the defense of Ousia by focusing on the collective security instead of themselves and also focusing on believing that fighting in defense of Ousia was the highest pleasure and greatest indulgence. Therefore, Yumen had to keep watchful eyes over those doors not only to maintain peace and order but also to keep the planet safe. As one Yumen put it, "It may have been better to not tell Yumen to keep the doors secure than to tell them and trigger the desire for experimenting with different open-door scenarios." As a result, the Yumen pushed the boundaries to see the effects of opening the doors to different degrees. Some opened the doors just enough for them to stick a hand out and wave to friends; this was representative of experimenting with the drug Plesordol. Others opened the doors just enough to stick their heads out; this was representative of the early days of addiction. Others, like those on Broadway Street, swung the doors wide open; this was representative of the drug completely controlling Yumen. Those who opened the doors developed certain social and health problems. Yumen began to complain of the lab syndrome. Yumen afflicted with this syndrome had very unhealthy appetites. They developed bigger stomachs and bigger heads than the rest of Yumen population; this led to serious mental health problems that affected the quality of their decisions and, by extension, the effective functioning of their brains, which were the trigger mechanisms of their weapons systems. Similarly, Yumen who habitually indulged in high dosage levels of Plesordol thought and behaved as if the sky above and the ground beneath had switched positions; for them, there were no stars but stones and there was no Sun but sticks. Therefore, they walked with their eyes fixed to the ground, avoiding the heavens. Ousians referred to this condition as the sky-avoidance syndrome.

The Yumen who held on to a Sunless Ousia argued with other Yumen so passionately about its nonexistence and significance that, when some later accepted that the Sun existed, they had mentally stripped it of its size and power. Though this cultural climate took over Ousia like wildfire, some Yumen ordered their lives to avoid being infected by the syndrome. The sky-avoidance syndrome with its tendency to keep its victims' heads bowed down instead of looking up was of great concern to most Yumen because it affected their level of alertness. The affected Yumen lost their strength and power and the skill sets that made them exceptional fighters and defenders of Ousia. As more and more Yumen became affected, the numerical and technical strength of Ousia's fighting force began to dwindle causing unaffected Yumen to voice what had long been a concern in the Ousian communities; that is, Yumen will test the waters if the control of the doors is entirely in their hands, and the enemy will eventually walk through the open doors reducing Ousia's fighting force to mere shadows.

After a long moment of reflection, Sunia sat up and looked toward the western skies of Plesorhub. He saw dark clouds sprinting toward the Sun and plant their claws on the face of the Sun. Immediately, Ousia erupted with sounds of drums; almost everyone came out with their talking drums and beat them passionately. In Ousia, whenever stygian clouds obscured the rays of the Sun, Yumen interpreted the phenomenon as a fight between the nameless and invisible enemy, who was believed to be the chief orchestrator of all evil and disorder in Ousia, and the Sun. To show their solidarity for the Sun, they beat their talking drums in a fast, double-stroke, seven-roll rhythm. As they beat their talking drums, they believed the sound and rhythm discharged vibrations of victory or peace into the atmosphere, forcing the dark clouds to retreat and enabling the Sun to grin again signaling a victory of good over evil, order over chaos. Ousians loved the rhythm of the talking drums; they shook their heads and tapped their feet to the beat though they could not dance because they lacked flexibility. After thirty minutes of ritual drumming, the clouds lifted in surrender, whipped by the thousands of seven-stroke beats across Ousia. They turned around and sprinted back to their hiding place causing Ousians to break out into singing. Their voices, filled with ecstatic emotions, drowned the quiet mountains of Ousia in the seas of rapturous jubilation, forcing a broad smile on the face of Sunia.

After this event, Sunia stood up, dusted himself off, and took off jogging downhill toward the center of Sunupsville. This time he had an additional weight on his mind pushing him downhill as he thought of the six men and the mysterious strangers of Broadway Street. This triggered pain in his knees, and he sought to slow down his momentum, but the joy of the triumph of order over chaos took the bite out of the pain.

When he got home, he went straight to his desk in his study room. He reached for the envelope containing pictures of enemy infiltrators; he displayed them on his desk and looked at them closely to see if they matched any of the twelve strangers he had seen on Broadway Street. After looking at the pictures intensively, Sunia whispered to himself, "Three of these faces look a lot like three among the twelve strangers I saw on Broadway Street. I wish I could remember all their faces. I wonder if Soggy knows anything about those guys! I need to talk to Soggy and glean information about these strangers."

CHAPTER 2

Enemy Infiltration from Another Planet

There is a baby monster in every Yumen craving for the right diet. When it is fed the right food, it grows to a giant monster and controls its host.

Soggy held onto the table and started to push himself into a standing position, but he staggered and fell back into his chair. "Hey, guys! I have to go home now," he said. "Okay, let's try this again," Soggy mumbled. He held on to the chair, mustered all the energy he could, and pushed himself up. Again, he fell back into his chair.

"Buzia does not want you to go home; each time you try to stand up, the chair like a magnet, sucks you back right into its lap!" whispered Natasi. "Let me get you a taxicab to take you home, but don't forget Deesix will swing by tomorrow to see you for an important discussion." Natasi stopped a grey electric sedan shaped like a frog. The driver pulled over to the edge of the road close to Soggy. He pressed a button, and the right door opened. Then the back seat, supported by two strong metal brackets, slid out twelve feet to the right, positioning itself over the gutter to where Soggy was sitting. Four metal legs popped out from under the seats and rested on the ground to provide support for the seat. Natasi helped Soggy out of his chair and into the seat of the vehicle. After Soggy sat down on the chair he was automatically buckled up. The driver pressed another button, and the seat lifted about two feet above the ground. The four supporting legs slid back to their positions under the seat, the seat slid back into the vehicle, and the door closed. "Tomorrow! Tomorrow! Don't forget the meeting with Deesix tomorrow," Natasi yelled at Soggy as the vehicle drove off.

The driver dropped Soggy right in front of his house. Soggy staggered into his house, threw his tired and drugged body on the couch at exactly midnight, and slept like a baby.

Thereafter, Natasi and his team shook hands with the five remaining Yumen, bade them good-bye, and walked across the street to the Slavking building.

Back in their station at the Slavking Building, General Natasi asked his eleven operatives, "Did you see the guy who waved at us while we were hanging out with—I mean disarming—the six Yumen down the road? He looked like someone who could pose a great threat to our mission."

"That's right Natasi," replied his second-in-command, General Deesix. "I am glad you brought this up because the image of that Yumen has never left my mind. I have seen a lot of Yumen from our base in Plusia and up-close since we arrived on this mission, but that guy is different. He exudes great power. He seems laser-focused on his purpose to defend Ousia, and he exudes enormous strength. When we asked Soggy and his friends if they knew who the guy was, they said they didn't know what we were talking about. All they had seen was the shadow of a man."

"Deesix! This is awesome! Remember I told you guys there is a baby monster in every Yumen craving for the right diet. When it is fed the right food, it grows into a giant monster and controls its host. The Plesordol drugs and Friskey-Six wine seem to be the right food, and they are having the desired effect on Yumen. Before the infiltration and neutralization timeframe of our mission expires, thousands of Yumen will have lost their purpose and will run around with defective Lous. Seeing Yumen as shadows will make it easy for our few recruits among them to shoot at other Yumen thinking they are shooting shadows. Meanwhile, I want you to find out everything there is to know about the guy who waved at us. But let us never forget who we are: we are the best warriors any planet could dream of, and all the enemies that ever stood against us have turned to dust!"

"Well said, Natasi!" said Deesix. "I have an appointment to meet up with Soggy tomorrow at the Buzia night club. I will press him to give me relevant information on this guy."

At this point, they heard a sudden loud screeching sound from the roof of the Slavking building. "Shush!" whispered Natasi. Then he placed his index finger on his thick lips signaling his team to be quiet. "Did you hear that loud screeching sound?" he asked his warriors.

"Yes, I did. It sounded like someone fired a gun," replied Deesix.

"Deesix! What is the difference between the sound of Pop music, a gunshot, and that of a Barred Owl?"

"Worthy General! They all sound like gunshot to a seasoned Plusia warrior," replied Deesix.

"Agreed! However, what I heard from the roof of the building, sounded like a Barred Owl, and I consider it a signal to go to bed. Goodnight Comrades!"

"Goodnight General," answered each of his warriors. Then they all shook hands, bade each other goodnight and went into their rooms.

Soggy woke up six o'clock the next morning with the word *Plusia* on his mind and the word *Ousia* hovering in the background. He stared at his bedroom ceiling as he tried to recollect the events of the day before. "Was it Plusia or Ousia?" Soggy questioned himself as he wiped his face with both hands as if wiping the sleep off his face. "Plusia! Pluisa! I am pretty sure I saw Plusia!" He tried hard to remember the word written on Natasi's T-shirt the day before. Soggy lifted himself and sat on the edge of the bed as he contemplated his trip to Broadway Street the day before. Then he whispered "Plusia!" several times. He remembered faintly seeing the word *Plusia* on Natasi's T-shirt, but he wondered if he'd seen the word *Ousia* instead. "I am pretty sure I saw the word *Plusia*. I am going to head over to the Museum of War History and research everything on Plusia." Soggy spoke out aloud to himself as a way of convincing himself and marshaling his energies for the task ahead.

At the museum, Soggy combed the entire library of books and files in search of information on Plusia. Finally, he stumbled on a book titled *The History and People of Plusia*. This book described Plusia as a planet of dancing warriors called Darkneys. According to the book, Darkneys were very tall warriors who fought extremely well at freezing temperatures. Their heights ranged from six foot five to nine feet. The smallest of them weighed at least three hundred pounds. Their bodies were comprised of a flexible polyurethane material, and they were fitted for any kind of warfare. The polyurethane served as a bulletproof mechanism against light weapons. Darkneys had two hands and two feet just like Yumen. Their heads, however, were far bigger. They had either one or two eyes the size of tennis balls, and they could see through every material object unless they were blinded by extreme sunlight. The hair on their heads was white signifying—according to Plusia's culture—longevity, wisdom, and dominance.

Darkneys lived on Plusia, a planet that was much closer to the Sun than planet Ousia. This was a planet dressed around its chest in mountains consisting of large grey impregnable boulders. There was a brown skirt of dust around its waist. The mountains stood majestically over towns in Plusia echoing the words of her ancient warriors about the indomitable spirit of the planet. Planet Plusia had a very little plant or animal life. The landscape was littered with thousands of green lakes. The buildings were mostly unpainted and made of red clay bricks that had been baked in fire. The roads were dusty; in fact, almost everything on planet Plusia—even the eyebrows and hands of most Darkneys—was covered in dust. Interestingly, Plusia was nicknamed Land of Warriors because the military council trained everyone in Plusia in one of her prestigious military schools. There were raised the finest warriors capable of defeating any army on any battlefield.

Plavar was the king of Plusia. He was advised by a council of twenty-four nine-star military generals led by General Natasi, —aka Deenine—as chairman of the military council. The council was tasked with the responsibility of not only advising the king, but also supervising the administration of the three military academies.

The School of Cobra Rangers was responsible for training students in gorilla or hand-to-hand combat specifically for land defense. It was headed by the nine-star General Deesix. The notable weapons in their arsenal were the Broadway Lightening Missiles (BLM) and the Cobra Poison Propelled Stinger (CPPS). The BLMs were long-range rocket-propelled missiles that delivered conventional weapons with lethal payloads; they were fast as lightning, accurate, and deadly in their delivery. The CPPSs were specially designed hand-held stinger launchers that delivered explosive stingers the size of footballs. Darkneys designed them to do the job of short-range ballistic missiles with mega payloads that could cut through hard substances like rock and metals.

The School of Marine Defense was responsible for training students to become warriors specifically for sea defense. It was headed by nine-star General Synke. This squadron had a fleet of two thousand Red Dust destroyers. These combatant ships were designed for naval warfare and were equipped with six massive guns in front and six in the rear.

The Jupiter Squadron Military Academy was responsible

for training students as defenders of Plusia's airspace. It was led by nine-star General Jupiter. They had in their arsenal hundreds of Plusia Crow999 Interplanetary Jets, each with four inbuilt torpedo launchers. The four torpedoes could be discharged simultaneously at the press of a button. These black jets were shaped like crows. They issued a great deal of noise, which struck fear in the hearts of enemies.

The one notable characteristic of Darkneys who graduated from the military academies was their inability to think independently for themselves because the heads of the military academies determined what they thought. The graduates were programmed by the military institutions to think a certain way, which according to the military elite, had the added advantage of easy control, which they considered critical to Plusia's military success. The coat of arms of Plusia consisted of the image of a short-faced bear with a dead cheetah in its mouth. These words written across the top: "Strength, speed, and subjugation."

In Plusia, each generation was named after a body part of the national animal, the short-faced bear. The first generation of Darkneys were represented by the head of the short-faced bear. They were dubbed the builders and were the founding fathers of Plusia. They built an intricate road system along with bridges connecting hundreds of mountains. They dug deep beneath the surface of the ground to lay down tracks for underground trains. They built the nation's communication infrastructure and transformed desert lands of Plusia to arable lands that fed its entire population. The next generation were represented by the eyes. They were the inventors. This was the era in the planet's history when they discovered the nano eye implant technology. A nano chip planted in one or both eyes enabled people to spy and track the military progress of other planets thousands of miles away, especially Planet Ousia. They built interplanetary vehicles that flew at the speed of light, and communication devices that eavesdropped on other planets. The eye generation added sophistication and efficiency to what the founding fathers had built. The next generation were represented by the stomach. They were the consumers, and they came after the eye generation. They were hungry for instant success to satisfy their growing appetites; they hated work but enjoyed spending. The stomach generation felt no obligation to the next generation. Blinded by a belief that Planet Plusia was headed for a cataclysmic war with distant enemies, they lived as if they were the last generation, consuming everything that had previously been saved up for the future. The next generation were represented by the feet. They were the warrior dancers. This was the generation that burned the history books and rewrote Plusia's history using musical notes.

They danced before fighting a battle and after losing a battle. They danced on the lines between pleasure and work. They danced on dusty floors and on tables and beds meant to hold personal and national balance sheets. It was a dance of power and passion; therefore, there were no hallowed grounds or private spaces. The rules were fluid on the dance floors, and many times the dance was dusty. The dancers closed their eyes and blocked their ears so they could dance without rules or rhythm. Plusia's population of warriors danced on the dancefloors of the future. Their steps were deliberately hard. They stomped on the glue that held the community together and trampled the foundation of norms.

Sometimes the dance was disharmonious. The moves were razor sharp, leaving the audience reeling from applause to shock. Some didn't like the dance but joined in, not just so they could not be branded misfits, but because the dance increased their level of mental alertness and energized them to fight better.

The dance started with few Darkneys every evening at six o'clock. Slowly but surely, the whole of Plusia joined in into the "carnival of the dusty dance." When Plusia danced, a large amount of dust rose into the atmosphere and made its way, eventually, into the eyes of the Sun, forcing it to blink several times before taking a short involuntary nap. In the third year of the dance carnival, a highly infectious disease called brown lungs broke out. This disease of the dusty lungs wiped out close to half a million Darkneys.

Soggy read the history book for a long time, taking copious notes to help him retain the information in his mind. As he turned over the information in his mind, he wondered if the word *Plusia* on Natasi's T-shirt had anything to do with the Planet Plusia he has just read about. "Is Natasi's T-shirt a show of planetary allegiance or is it just an ordinary T-shirt worn by an ordinary being?" he asked himself. This information and rumors of strange beings in town helped heighten his desire to meet with Deesix.

Later that day, Deesix met Soggy at the Buzia night club, and they both went into the private lounge. Deesix introduced himself again as a businessman from the island of Ossam off the coast of Ousia. His intent was to invest in various sectors of the economy, especially entertainment. Deesix ordered two bottles of apple juice—one for Soggy and one for himself. The bartender on duty brought the bottles of juice along with two highball glasses. He poured the juice into the glasses. Deesix grabbed his glass and took a long sip. He put the glass back on the table and ran his left hand from the top of his face down to his silver beard. Then he looked at Soggy in the eye. "Hey, Soggy, it was nice hanging out with you guys yesterday. We had a wonderful time," exclaimed Deesix. He picked up his glass, took another sip, and beamed with a smile meant to be contagious.

But Soggy did not smile back; neither did he drink his juice because his research materials had filled him with suspicion and imprisoned his smiles. "Did you say you guys are businessmen from the island of Ossam?" enquired Soggy as his eyes scanned the eyes and body language of Deesix for clues of deceit.

"That's right, Soggy. We invest in hotels, night clubs, and sports teams. I am so excited about our partnership to take our business to the next level," replied Deesix. The seasoned operative acted very professionally. His looks, posture, and body language wrapped his package of lies in a disposition of truth and left no hole for Soggy to peep through. This melted the ice of suspicion in Soggy's mind and replaced it with an attitude of trust. "We are still looking for more business partners and workers across Ousia to help manage our many businesses. Hey, Soggy! Do you remember the guy who waved at us yesterday by the roadside? I have a good feeling he would make a good partner."

"I remember nothing, Deesix. I was too drunk and drugged up. The only thing I remember was the word on Natasi's T-shirt."

"What was it?"

"Plusia! The word *Plusia* was written on Natasi's T-shirt, and that word won't stop ringing in my mind. With all the rumors of strangers in town to destabilize Ousia, I cannot help but think you guys are from Planet Plusia. Tell me, are you from planet Plusia?"

"That name sounds familiar; I read about it when I was in junior high school, and it is still fresh in my mind because my teacher back then, Mr. Wise, asked me to stand up during a geography class so he could use me to describe the physical characteristics of people from Plusia. According to him, I look just like someone from Plusia. The fact is, Soggy, I am not from Plusia. I am from the island of Ossam," replied Deesix, effortlessly sustaining his smile of innocence.

At this point, Soggy lifted the glass to his lips and smiled back causing Deesix to order more bottles of apple juice. "I am glad you chose this part of Ousia as your investment destination; this will create more jobs for folks in this community and boost the economy of Ousia as a whole," babbled Soggy as he gulped more juice down into his stomach.

"Tell me, from a worker's point of view, how is the Buzia night club doing."

"Deesix! There is no night club in all of Broadway Street and Ousia that is defining the lifestyle of Yumen like Buzia. As soon as we step our feet on Broadway Street and into Buzia, we completely forget who we are. It is as if a strange force from another planet that's antithetical to Ousia and disruptive to the culture of her fighting force takes over us. We pack this club full of Yumen every single day. In a nutshell, business is good for the owners of Buzia and good for the economy, but bad for the spirit and culture of Ousia."

"Interesting!" said Deesix. "I never saw it that way, but it's true that this planet has gone through deep cultural shifts. I never for once thought of the effect of that change on the quality of her fighting force. Ousia will pull through as she has always done. Sometimes she has to get it wrong to get it right."

Soggy looked at his wrist watch and said, "Hey, Deesix, we will have to continue this conversation another time; I have to go back to work." Then he quickly emptied the last of his juice into his mouth.

Soggy and Deesix shook hands and walked out of the lounge. Soggy walked toward the stage and disappeared behind the thick black curtain.

Deesix left Buzia and rushed back to the Slavking Building across the street to tell the rest of the team the result of his meeting with Soggy. "Natasi! Natasi! Where are you?" shouted Deesix.

"I am in the storeroom," replied Natasi. Deesix rushed to the storeroom. Natasi was packing boxes of Plesordol so his men could distribute it to agents the next day. "Welcome back, Deesix. How did your meeting with Soggy go?" enquired Natasi.

"Natasi! Did you know Soggy picked up the name on the T-shirt you wore the other day and asked if we were from Plusia?"

"Really? What did you say to him?"

"I told the lies we told yesterday and cemented them with another lie! Lying has become so natural to me that, when I lie, I feel I am telling the truth."

"You are a true warrior! Plusia's warrior! We must take over Ousia and make it our home at all costs. In doing so, we will use every available weapon including lies. Summon the other team members to a brief meeting, and let go over the king's command and the plans of the warfare council." Deesix pressed the tiny bell on the table by the left side of Natasi, and immediately the other ten team member formed a perfect semicircle in front of Natasi. They bowed their heads. "Heads up, comrades! It has come to our notice that Yumen are suspecting we are behind the recent social and health problems in Ousia. I encourage you to be very professional in dealing with them and keep your identity secret. The moment to strike is fast approaching, but first, we must degrade and disarm as many Yumen as possible through our social and cultural weapons. I want you to stay the course, make a thousand Soggys out of the fighting force of Ousia. Divide them and drug them up until we weaken Ousia from within. Then we will strike with all the military might of Plusia. Warriors of Plusia, let's get to work!"

CHAPTER 3

Sunia and the Army of Zimen

They have the fire of the Sun in their eyes, and they are alive to the singular purpose of defending Ousia.

After a long period of gathering, studying, and compiling intelligence, Sunia dressed in blue jeans and a black T-shirt. He donned sunglasses and a baseball cap, tilting it to the front so that the bill covered part of his face. For a man mostly seen in public in a suit, the outfit was a fine disguise. He took a taxicab to Broadway Street to look for Soggy but was shocked to see the number of Yumen without golden hats on the street and in the nightclubs bumping into each other on the dance floors.

Sunia took some time to check out some nightclubs on Broadway Street and was stunned by what he saw. He saw Yumen sitting on the floors of some nightclubs reeling under the influence of drugs, Yumen without pants dancing until they passed out, and Yumen with eyes that betrayed a bottomless void longing for power and purpose. Sunia walked into the Buzia night club and looked around to see if he could find Soggy. He pulled one worker aside. "Hey, sir," Sunia asked the worker, "I am looking for Soggy. Do you know where I can find him?"

"Oh! You are looking for Soggy the bartender! What can I get you, sir? We have drugs that will take you to another planet and back to Ousia in no time, and we will celebrate your arrival back in Ousia with our finest Friskey-Six wine to make your heart extremely glad," replied the worker.

"Thank you. I want nothing. I just want to see Soggy."

"No problem. Hang on. Let me see if I can find him for you." The man walked to the side of the stage and disappeared behind a thick black curtain. After a few minutes, Soggy and the guy walked out. They both stood by the curtain while the worker pointed to where Sunia was standing. Soggy walked toward Sunia. "Sir, what can I do for you?" he asked.

Sunia pulled him aside and spoke quietly into his ear. "I am Sunia. We need to talk, but this is not a good place. Take this card. This is the address of the place I want us to meet. Is tomorrow a good time to meet?"

"No, my brother. I will be very busy tomorrow. Let make it this same time the day after tomorrow.

"Great! See you then." Sunia quickly walked out of Buzia. He hailed a taxicab, sat at the backseat, buried his head between his knees, and pondered the future of Ousia in the face of sudden cultural declension seeking to divide the planet and decimate her fighting force. *We have a crisis on our hands*, he thought. *And its gathering pace. If we don't act now, Ousia will cease to exist. The name Ousia had always struck fear into the hearts of her enemies, and those who contemplated attacking her were paralyzed by fear because every single Yumen is a skillful fighter. However, the enemy we are facing is different and strong—though a great many Yumen may regard them as the weakest—because they destroy fighters from within by taking the desire to fight out of them. That enemy is a little white pill—Pleserdol. It is the size of a nickel and is wrapped in a sinister plan. Whoever is supplying it does not like Yumen!*

The vehicle stopped, and Sunia walked to his home at the base of the mountain of Sunupsville. Once inside, he walked straight to his desk to continue working on his pieces of intelligence. After long hours of work, Sunia went to bed. That night he could not sleep. He tossed and turned on his bed as images of the Yumen on Broadway Street flashed through his mind. The next day, he went back to his desk and worked long hours with the sole conviction that the future of Ousia depended on the outcome of this work. *I must connect dots and fill the gaps, if there are any, on these pieces of intelligence on the twelve men on Broadway Street and their relationship to the security and social problems of Ousia. I must find out the source of the qualitative decline of Ousia's fighting force.* He said these words to himself anytime he came to a dead end or faced mountains of challenges in his search for vital intelligence. That day, he worked till midnight, taking only a few breaks to push liquid and food down into his stomach. Finally, he threw his tired body on the couch.

He woke up at seven o'clock the next morning and drove his white Jeep to the Grapevine Restaurant in the center of Sunupsville to meet with Soggy. He pulled into the parking spot in front of the restaurant, entered the restaurant, and sat by the window close to the street so he would be able to see Soggy when he arrived. A few hours later, Soggy pulled up in a black sedan taxicab. As soon as Soggy's feet touched the ground, Sunia walked outside to meet him, gave him a warm handshake, and ushered him into the restaurant. They sat in the extreme corner of what was known as the overflow room. That day business was slow, and no one else was in the overflow room.

"Yumen in this part of Ousia are different," exclaimed Soggy.

"What do you mean?" asked Sunia.

"They have the fire of the Sun in their eyes, and they are alive to the singular purpose of defending Ousia. It shows in their gait and their words. And you know what? They remind me of the fathers of Ousia. Sunia! Sunupsville reminds me of the past when Yumen lived within certain accepted boundaries and fought against shiftless standards. I wish to go back to the past, but my present condition feels better."

"Soggy, I am glad you are not seeing shadows today. Interestingly, this means you must have noticed that the Yumen in Plesorhub and other parts of Ousia are losing their fighting edge and undoing the bonds that made us one."

"Sunia, we are dead. The fighting force of Ousia in that part of the planet is dead, but the reality is we enjoy being dead because dead people have nothing to worry about. Obviously, there is a cultural wave sweeping Ousia that is different from what Yumen are used to. There seems to be no going back to the past, and I fear that the current momentum will divide this planet and lead to its takeover."

"Talking of takeover, do you remember the day I jogged past you and the other Yumen on Broadway Street?"

"Sure, I remember vividly."

"Who were the other twelve people who joined you later?"

"Oh! They are businessmen from the island of Ossam on Ousia, and they are here to invest in some business ventures. Those guys are creating a lot of job opportunities for the inhabitants of Ousia."

"Yeah! That is what I heard. Do you know their names?"

"I know the names of the two leaders of the group, but I don't know the rest. One is Natasi and the other is Deesix."

"Wow! Strange names. They sound like ranks in the military establishment of a distant planet."

"Sunia, those guys look strange."

"Yeah, they look strange! There are many night clubs springing up on Broadway Street; however, what amazed me, and which is new and strange, is not just their number but also the amount of patronage they are getting from Yumen. Do you know who owns the nightclubs?"

"I don't know who owns any of them," said Soggy. "My friends told me Buzia is owned by a consortium of companies, but in reality, the identity of the owners is unknown."

"Tell me about the drug Plesordol," said Sunia. "Do you have any idea where it is coming from and who is supplying it?"

"Nobody knows exactly where it is coming from, but rumor has it that it's coming from the island of Ossam."

"Does that mean that Natasi and Deesix have something to do with it?"

Soggy sipped a bit of water, looked at Sunia, blinked his eyes several times, and whispered, "I think it a possibility, but I am not sure. Sunia why are you asking all these questions? Is there anything I need to know?"

"Soggy, I have so much concern for Ouisa. I don't like the direction this planet is going; therefore, I am looking for answers that will change the script and make Yumen like yourself the fiercest fighters you once were. I believe the future of this planet depends on it. You were one of the finest fighters in Ousia, but I am afraid you are losing your power. Broadway Street is destroying your weapons and fighting skills, and it is doing the same to many other Yumen. I am looking for possible causes. When was the last time you did the Sun-concentration exercise?"

"It's been ages," said Soggy. "My job as a bartender at Buzia is so demanding, and it leaves me no time for anything. Sunia, I want to spend a good amount of time gazing at that ball of fire to chase out the coldness within me, but I feel a strong pull toward Broadway Street even on my off days, and I succumb easily. Look at you! You seem to be unmoved and untouched by this ebb and flow of unhealthy social events and culture war. Tell me, Sunia, what type of metal is your chest made of?"

"Soggy, I understand that feeling."

"You do?" asked Soggy with a look of surprise on his face.

"Yes! I feel the same way. There is a Broadway Street in all of us. That is why I don't shop on Broadway Street. By the way, let me tell you a secret."

Soggy leaned forward, turned his left ear in the direction of Sunia's face, sat still, and quieted himself to chase out every noise on his mind and block out every noise in the environment. "Tell me the secret," he whispered softly in order not to wake up the noise he had put to sleep.

"Every good fighter has to learn to fight and conquer himself if he wants to conquer others," replied Sunia.

Soggy leaned back in his chair, breathed heavily, glanced quickly at Sunia, and looked at the table in front of him intensely for thirty seconds before he said, "Those words mean a lot to me, especially coming from your metal chest. Knowing that I am not alone in this struggle will put me on the path of finding another sea beside Whiskey-Six or Plesordol in which to drown my frustrations."

"Soggy! Move to Sunupsville. Change your environment a little and fan the dying embers of your purpose as a fighter."

"Sunia, thanks for the good sentiment. I have never thought of moving to Sunupsville, but I will think about it."

"Thank you so much for taking time off your busy schedule to talk to me," said Sunia.

"No! thank you for taking time off your busy schedule to talk to me. I greatly appreciate it," replied Soggy.

Sunia and Soggy shook hands and walked out of the restaurant. After they bade each other good-bye, Soggy walked into a waiting vehicle. He waved at Sunia as the vehicle sped off. After the vehicle disappeared, Sunia entered his Jeep and drove home. When he got home, he looked through his file containing intelligence on Plusia to see if he could match the names in the file to the names Soggy had given him, but none of the names matched. This triggered a lot of questions in the mind of Sunia. "Who is Natasi? Who is Deesix? Could this be General Deenine from Planet Plusia? If Plusia were to attack Ousia, the best candidate to lead the attack will be General Deenine," whispered Sunia to himself.

Later that day, Sunia compiled all the intelligence he and his men had been working on and sent the file to King Heddy Wisemen with the warning "Ousia is under attack by secret agents from Plusia, and swift action is needed immediately to stop it. Action will also reverse the effect of the infiltration in order to prevent the possible division and decimation of her fighting force."

When King Wiseman got the message, he summoned Sunia to a meeting immediately to discuss the details of his findings. In less than three hours, Sunia was at the king's court. Right on the table in front of the king was a copy of the report. Sunia bowed his head three times before the king and declared, "I pay you homage, my king. You called for your servant."

"Welcome to my court, worthy captain, son of Ousia, and head of my intelligence division." The king offered Sunia a seat; he pointed to the report before him with his thick index finger and said, "I have read the summary of the report. I want you to tell me, in person, all you know about the enemy infiltration of my planet."

Sunia said to the king, "My king, I ask your permission to stand to talk about my findings so I can run immediately to execute your command when you make your decision."

"Granted! Now tell me the details of your findings."

"My King, a disease of epidemic proportions broke out in Planet Plusia about a year ago that killed a lot of its inhabitants. Consequently, the king of Plusia and his military advisers asked their chief shaman about the cause of the pandemic. The shaman spilled the entrails of an animal, as was the custom, and saw in them an image of what looked like the Sun. He therefore blamed the disease on the Sun. He told the inhabitants of Plusia to move to another planet or risk being wiped out by the Sun. The shaman, after consulting the oracle, advised them to choose a planet—specifically Planet Ousia—that was perfectly positioned away from the Sun. They should work to make it dark and sunless. According to the shaman, the Sun would hide its face if they could get Yumen to take off their golden hats and start a rebellion against the Sun by not observing the Sun-concentration exercise. This would spread division among Yumen and usher them into a state of coldness, which would result in extreme bodily weakness. This would enable the Darkneys to kill them and take over the planet.

"As a result of this oracle, King Plavar and his Plusia military council sent an elite group of twelve warriors drawn from all three branches of the military to lead the initial infiltration and neutralization of Ousia's fighting force through an operation called Broadway Military Warfare. To provide organization and better implementation of their plans, they set up headquarters in the middle of Broadway Street in the city of Plesorhob and named it the Slavking Building. Subsequently, the Broadway military council established the Buzia night club to act as a vehicle to poke holes in the culture of purpose and power in Yumen. This was the most notable of all the nightclubs and was on Broadway Street across the street from the Slavking Building.

"My King, the Buzia night club buzzes like a well-fed bee. It sings from dawn to dusk forcing even unwilling Yumen to dance the dusty dance of Plusia. The sounds and lyrics of her songs and the vibration of a thousand feet on her dance floor have a rare magnetic pull that sucks in passers-by, especially the many gullible Yumen, through its revolving doors. The dusty dance starts with a violent circular gyration of the mid part of the Yumen body; the dancers then open both hands wide apart as if surrendering to the direction of the wind. Then, with a fast and hard three steps forward, they raise their right feet high and then stomp their feet, slicing through the air. Then the dancers make a sudden stop, move six steps backward and then start the circular gyration of their hips again. As the dancers slice through the air during their backward steps, the stomping of their feet pushes the dust-filled air into their Dobies, thus increasing their size and weight. These Broadway Street–addicted Yumen danced as if they have taken flexibility pills made in military laboratories of Plusia. They have discovered their dance moves. Often, after the Buzia dance sessions, most of her patrons end up being reconditioned to think with their feet and walk back home on their heads. The common saying is, 'Feet to Buzia, heads home!'

"One Yumen who experienced the dance said these words to me, 'When we were filled with dust-filled air through the Buzia dance, we lost control of our identity. Our power dwindled fast, and our purpose was strangled to death. Like soccer balls, we were at the mercy of highly skillful dusty feet.' To introduce chaos, the council gave orders to shoot thousands of Yumen with dark-impulse trigger capsules (DITCs), weapons in the arsenal of the Jupiter Squadron used to control enemies from the outside. Yumen exposed to the DITC are no longer in possession of their impulses but are conditioned to act out the dark impulses of the Broadway forces. The capsule released chemicals into the

Doby, infected Yumen with, among many other detriments, the lab syndrome that causes enormous tension in the head thus suppressing the natural functions of the brain. This caused affected Yumen to act like mental zombies.

"The most damaging warfare tactic, which will leave a lasting effect on the social culture and lifestyle of Ousia if unchecked, is cranial warfare, also known as negative warfare. It was so named because the Darkney warriors direct the missiles at the left side of the heads of the Yumen to introduce and maintain a zigzag, or lead scribbler, thinking patterns that originated in Plusia. These are meant to replace the vertical thinking pattern of Ousians. Darkneys call it a zigzag thinking pattern because they don't think in terms of ups or downs, a center, and circumference as we do. Their thinking pattern follows that of a lead scribbler who scribbles intelligible or unintelligible characters and gives them his meaning expecting Darkneys to accept and live by the meaning because of the reputation and authority of the lead scribbler.

"In Plusia, Darkneys call the lead scribblers high priests of the cranial hemispheres, and their job is to create a planet of mass thinkers. The Darkneys in authority created a homogeneous thinking climate by shaping the thinking pattern of ordinary Darkneys. According to the Broadway operatives, introducing a zigzag thinking pattern in Ousia would either close the gates of the mind and leave just one gate for the high priest of the cranial hemispheres, or add many rounded gates with different shades of color creating a generation of merry-go-round thinkers, thus imposing a state of confusion. In the ensuing climate of mental fuzziness and confusion, they expect Yumen to go down the tubes of emptiness with their lenses tied tightly around their necks. When this happens, the disoriented Yumen will push the mental eject button of the high-speed merry-go-round and fall at the altar of the high priest, or they will opt for a less-expensive or familiar island of ideas, which will end up destroying their chances to prepare for the ongoing battle. If there are Yumen who do not fall for this tactic, the Broadway warfare council from Plusia will encourage them into an ostrich mindset of burying their heads in the comfort of a predictable and familiar Ousia. This will allow the cold and dusty tentacles of Darkneys to wrap around their heads and hearts resulting in the numbing of their senses to a higher and hostile reality. This will make them look like little children with sunglasses in a dark cave."

When Sunia ended his intelligence report, King Wiseman stood up walked to the window overlooking the city of Plesorhub. He gazed at the city for a while and then walked back to Sunia. "Interesting! Very interesting! Thank you, Captain, for your pains and insight. However, do you really think there are fools on this planet or any other planet that will dare to face the fighting force of Ousia? Sunia, this planet is the greatest and will continue to be so. Who would want to fight a planet where every single inhabitant is a deadly weapon? I am convinced that Ousia will remain undefeated, and anyone who invades her does it at their own peril."

"My King, beside Darkney warriors, we are facing other enemies called Plesordol and Friskey-Six that survive missiles and bullets. And Ousia has never faced these enemies before. These enemies seem to be the first weapons in a plan to conquer Ousia. My King, we need new strategies to fight against these weapons, and time is running out. I plead with you, order your men to start a campaign to unite all Yumen under the flag of Ousia, and let all in Ousia take seriously the Sun-concentration exercise. Encourage them to keep their golden hats glued to their heads."

"Again, I want to say thank you for your dedication to the security of Ousia. Give me some time to study the report thoroughly. Meanwhile, I would like you to gather like-minded Yumen and start a campaign to unite all Yumen and get them battle ready and back to the Sun-concentration exercise," ordered king Wiseman.

Sunia bowed before the king and whispered, "Consider it done, my King!" Then he walked out of the palace and drove back to Sunupsville. Based on the king's directive, Sunia conferred with all Yumen and Zimen in Sunupsville, and they decided to organize a three-day boot camp to take place before the independent anniversary celebration of Ousia. Also, Sunia and his men decided that, to make it more effective, they would allow three weeks for the men to prepare and get the message through all the news media to every inhabitant of Ousia. Sunia chose Shepherds' Field, which was seven hundred and seventy-seven kilometers west of Plesorhub, as the venue. Additionally, he appeared in many television shows in Ousia to encourage Yumen to attend the boot camp so as to sharpen their fighting skills. He pleaded with them to watch out for suspicious activities and report such activities to the Bureau of National Intelligence.

One evening, Natasi turned on the television in his room and saw Sunia talking about the importance of the camp and encouraging people to attend. Natasi ran out of his bedroom and stood by the door to Deesix's room. He banged on the door screaming at the top of his voice, "Deesix! Deesix! Open the door! Turn your television to channel thirty-seven." Deesix opened the door and turned on the television. Natasi rushed in with fire in his eyes and pointed his thick, cold finger at Sunia on the television screen. "That's the Yumen who waved at us on Broadway Street! His name is Sunia, and he is the one leading the campaign to unite Yumen and polish their fighting skill through the Sun exercise. And guess what? To achieve that, he is organizing a three-day boot camp at Shepherds' Field."

"Yeah! That is the guy! That's him!" screamed Deesix, waking the other members of the team who were in their rooms having an evening of rest before heading out for the wholesale distribution of Plesordol to agents across Ousia. They all rushed out of their rooms toward the sound of the scream in Deesix's room. They saw the image of Sunia on the screen.

"I told you this guy looked like someone who would pose a serious threat to our mission," muttered Natasi. Then he grabbed his outer garment and tore it into three parts. He threw it on the floor and stomped on it with his right foot screaming, "So shall Ousia divide, and thereafter I will rest my foot on the neck of that goat call Sunia!"

"He is not just a goat, Natasi," said Deesix. "He is the Director of National Intelligence of Planet Ousia. We need to find out more about this guy. Soggy is working today, Natasi. Let's go over to Buzia and talk with him. I am sure he must have seen the message. However, before we leave this room, be a true Darkney and hide your anger and hate in the inner chamber of laughter. Let your smile and handshake be warm enough to dispel all forms of suspicion," exclaimed Deesix.

"It is done!" said Natasi. "Guys, we will be back. Deesix, let's go!" Natasi and Deesix walked out of the Slavking Building and walked across the footbridge to the other side of the road into Buzia, greeting every Yumen with broad smiles. That evening, Yumen conversation at Buzia centered around the boot camp. A few Yumen who advocated for unity and a return to high standards in the fighting force of Ousia expressed delight about the camp and hoped it would put Yumen back on the track of military prowess. However, most Yumen in Buzia and Broadway Street opposed the camp. Some discussion degenerated into heated arguments with fistfights.

Natasi and Deesix listened in for a short while and then pulled Soggy into a private lounge. "Soggy, what is all the argument about?" asked Deesix, pretending they don't know what was going on.

"Oh, that? It is about the boot camp announced by Sunia. He wants to bring all Yumen together under the singular purpose of defending Ousia against her enemies."

"Wow! That's very ambitious of him. Do you think he has what it takes to succeed?" asked Natasi.

"Oh yes! I have no doubt about his ability. That guy is a Zimen."

"Zimen? What's a Zimen?" asked Deesix.

"They are everything I am supposed to be, but I am not."

"What do you mean, Soggy?"

"Guys, we are now living in a different Ousia because of major culture shifts. Prior to the new Ousia, every inhabitant of Ousia was the ultimate soldier. They were well trained, physically fit all the time, mentally alert every second of the day, and always ready to defend Ousia. Every Yumen lived by the culture of military success; that is, they spent a lot of time sharpening their fighting skills and looked at the Sun periodically to harness its energy and add power to the chest portion of their Lous. Natasi! We were the wall around Ousia that touched the Sun."

"What do you mean by Lous? What is that?" Deesix interrupted Soggy.

"Let me show you something!" Soggy unbuttoned his shirt and exposed the metal chest and stomach portion of his body. He tried to signal the Lous through his brain. He wanted his brain to push the switch for the Doby doors to slide back and expose the Lous, but he did not have enough current to power the slide. This was due to his lack of Sun-concentration exercise. "The door to my Doby is not opening. Maybe the Lous is not receiving a signal from my brain. Guys, I am sorry I cannot demonstrate the capability of my Lous to you. This has happened to a lot of Yumen. They have disarmed us."

"That's okay, Soggy. Please continue your explanation of Zimen. Maybe you can show us another time."

"As I was saying, the forces of a strange culture from nowhere started sweeping through Ousia striping Yumen like me of their purpose and power. The Yumen who braved the cultural storm and maintained the standards and expectations of Ousia's fighting force are called Zimen. They form a tiny percentage of the total population of Ousia. Most of them live in Sunupsville. They are the most powerful force for good on this planet. They fight to defeat the enemies of Ousia and maintain social and cultural order. The most powerful Zimen are those who feed off the Sun consistently; this exercise polishes and empowers their Lous and transforms them into bodies of light that is destructive to the enemy. Also, the Sun food, as they called it, can weaponize their Lous and make them effective launchpads for their arsenals of destructive weapons.

"Natasi, no two Zimen are the same! Their various voltages determined their light intensity and their effectiveness to strike and destroy their targets. The higher the voltage—which is determined by their efficiency and time they spend sucking up the Sun's energy—the more powerful they are. A well-developed Lous-equipped Zimen can effectively fight off enemy forces. This is a quality that we ordinary Yumen, who have taken off our hats and opened the door to our Dobymine and Lousomin cells, have not nurtured. The other advantage they possess is the in-built enemy sensor at the center of their Lous. It is uniquely capable of detecting enemy invasion. Their Lous are surrounded by a boomerang shield mechanism that can melt down incoming enemy weapons or launch those enemy weapons—through their nano-second reaction launchpad device—back to the place of origin.

"However, the lack of Sun-concentration exercise deactivated the boomerang shield mechanisms, and some enemy cartridges will hit the Dobies. They will become lodged there, causing intense vibration, heavy suppression, and disconnection from the needed energy of the Sun, thus reducing the potency and effectiveness of their weapon systems. Also, a few highly Sun-fed Zimen have the power to glean intelligence from the enemy through devices on their Lous. Using this microsecond red-rays transmission capability, the Sun-connected Lous gathered valuable intelligence from enemy territories through the link between the Sun and their Lous. The Sun's rays were the actual intelligence conduit. The Sun picked up the intelligence and sent it through its rays to the Lous of a highly Sun-connected Zimen.

"Notably, the most lethal weapon in the chambers of Dobies of the Zimen is the sea, land, and air weapons trace destroyer (SLAWTAD). This weapon can destroy large-and small-scale moving and stationary weapons systems by tracing the launch origin of enemy weapons through inbuilt Sun-tracer technology. This technology enables the missile to quickly travel through the residue of smoke in the atmosphere and hit its target with deadly precision. It can then reroute itself to hit fast-moving targets.

"The most outstanding of all the Zimen is Sunia. He has high voltage and unmatched firepower in his Lous. Usually, his power spikes up to a maximum level as he lay on his back facing the heavens with his eyes consistently fixed on the Sun. Sunia spends countless hours looking at the Sun, sucking up its energy and cranking up the temperature of his Lous. Also, the dagger chamber in the Lous of this Sun warrior contains a sharp electric seme dagger that travels at the speed of light. It is propelled by the high-power voltage in his Lous and leaves behind a trail of pain and death. However, all of the weapons of Zimen are concealed by their Dobies and covered by layers of clothes to make them look ordinary and unsuspecting to the enemy. Natasi! Sunia is not just the Director of National Intelligence; he is the Captain of the army of Zimen," finished Soggy.

"Soggy, do you consider yourself a Zimen?" enquired Deesix.

"Nope! I consider myself a Yumen with the potential of becoming a Zimen."

Natasi cleared his throat and thanked Soggy for the opportunity to see, at least, his bare chest. He reached for Soggy's right hand and squeezed it softly. "It is always great talking to you, Soggy. Your insights on matters relating to Ousia are invaluable. Thanks for taking the pains to show us your metal chest. I will leave for the island of Ossam in few days, and I needed to see you before I leave, but Deesix and the other guys will still be around. If you need anything, don't hesitate to ask them. However, I hope whatever comes out of this boot camp and the tension surrounding it will make Ousia stronger and united," declared Natasi.

"Thanks for stopping to see me," said Soggy. "I wish you a safe trip, Natasi." Deesix and Natasi shook Soggy's hand, and they both walked out of the private lounge and out of Buzia to the Slavking Building.

On their way to the Slavking Building, Deesix turned to General Natasi and said, "I think Yumen have a design flaw. Their Lous should have been positioned on their hands, necks, or their legs instead of their chests."

"What do you mean?" enquired Natasi.

"I mean the center of that noble emotion—love—should never be weaponized."

"Deesix, every good warrior must go through his own funeral while he is alive. Have you done yours?"

"I was numbed the first day of military training and died the first time I killed."

"That means you don't have a heart. You have a design flaw, and I happen to be one of the designers."

"Natasi, I have never thought of it as a flaw, and if you think it's a flaw, it's a good flaw because, without it, Plusia would be a footnote on the pages of history."

"There is possibility I will die on this mission. I will be killed by a missile from the chest of a Yumen. That will be the most painful of all deaths. Deesix, I would rather be killed by your sword than by a sword from the heart of a Yumen"

"General Natasi, you are talking about possibilities of war that are impossible when the war is waged by determined Darkney warriors, the hungry short-faced bears of Plusia. By the way, don't forget that a Darkney warrior does not die."

When they reached the door of the building, they both stopped for a moment. Natasi turned to Deesix patted him on his shoulder and said, "My brother, fighting in defense of Plusia is immortality itself." Deesix opened the door, and as they both walked in, Natasi declared, "This mission is an open door to immortality."

Outside the Slaveking Building and elsewhere on the streets of Ousia, discussions about the boot camp raged on leading to a sharp divide in opinion within the Ousian population. On the day of boot camp, thousands of Yumen made their way to Shepherds' Field, and thousands more refused to attend. They agitated for an independent territory that would make provision for Yumen who preferred an alternative lifestyle. Two groups of agitators marched that day. The first group marched down Broadway Street shouting, "We don't need the Sun! We don't want the hat!" This group was comprised of the extremists who wanted nothing to do with the Sun-concentration exercise and loathed putting on the hat. They held placards high for Yumen to see. One placard read: "We are the Sun. Why should we put on the hat?" Another read: "We want a red bucket hat to provide shade against the Sun instead of a gold cone hat." The other group that marched that day was comprised of moderate Yumen who wanted the freedom to make their own choices and not be saddled by the rules of their fathers. Some of their placards read "We want the freedom to choose what we put on and what to look at. Nobody should tell us what to do." They marched from Broadway Street all the way to King Wiseman's palace singing and waving their placards as they went along and back to Broadway Street.

Interestingly, those who attended the boot camp came back with a strong resolve to unite the planet and preserve the culture of her fighting force. In their zeal to solve Ousia's problems, they reached out to other Yumen and encouraged them to join the campaign for power through the Sun-concentration exercise. Also, they flooded the media with images of Yumen on Plesordol, showing the drug's effect on the quality of Ousia's fighting force. These images were accompanied by the message to unite under the flag of Ousia. This led to more agitation, which led to the division of the planet into three regions: The Sunfuss Region, the Sunshun Region, and the Sunbond Region.

The Yumen who had discarded the golden hat disliked the Sun-concentration exercise and spoke negative things against the Sun moved to the coldest part of Ousia, the Sunfuss Region. The Yumen who ignored the Sun and put on their golden hats only when it was convenient lived in the Sunshun Region, which had a normal temperature of sixty degrees Fahrenheit. The Yumen and Zimen, most of whom had their golden hats glued to their heads and relished the exercise of gazing at the Sun, populated the Sunbond Region, which included Plesorhub and Sunupsville, the hottest part of Ousia.

In the early hours of the day exactly two weeks before Ousia's independence celebration, General Natasi called his eleven operatives into the conference room of the Slavking Building for a meeting. "Comrades! Short-faced bears of Plusia! This is the right time to roll out the next phase of the takeover plan. We have divided Ousia, and we have disarmed some Yumen. To further deepen the divide among Yumen, we must give them an Independence Day gift of missiles. Deesix, I want you to move the headquarters of our operations to the Sunfuss region before Independence Day. I am heading to Plusia to put together a battalion of warriors to launch an attack. We will kill as many Yumen as possible and start the process of taking over Ousia. Guys, let's stay the cause. We are winning!" Immediately after the meeting, A Plusia Crow999 interplanetary jet flew Natasi to Plusia.

CHAPTER 4

The Rearview Mirror of Plusia's War Campaign

I am saying fight your enemy as many times as possible until you defeat him. Fight him with your head, your guts, and your heart. Fight him with every ounce of your flesh and to the last drop of your blood.

Independence Day was the day Ousians celebrated their independence from the gods, and the Independence Day following the boot camp was the first independence celebration after the planet had been divided, but there were hopes among Zimen and some Yumen that the celebration would bring all factions together and unite the planet. Yumen came from all three regions of Ousia. The day started with an Ousian solidarity march by most Yumen down the eighty-kilometer Broadway Street of Plesorhub, then went north to Independence Avenue all the way to the

Independence Square, an open rectangular area the size of a soccer field.

Most of the Zimen who attended the celebration because they feared they would be attacked by Yumen opposed to the boot camp and the Sun-concentration exercise. They activated their boomerang shield mechanisms and went straight to Independence Square where they took their positions on the terrace. Independence Day was also a day for infusing a spirit of patriotism and hard work into all Ousians. The goal was to make Ousia the envy of the gods. Later, more Yumen made their way to Independence Square amidst fireworks and loud music.

There were special security features in Independence Square, including a missile-proof rectangular disc slide. At the press of a button, in microseconds, the circular surface on which events were organized would drop twenty feet below the surface of the square into an open basement. It would immediately be replaced by a missile-proof rectangular disc. Whenever important occasions were held in Independence Square in Ousia, dignitaries and guests occupied seats in the open fields while the terrace was occupied by armed Yumen who provided security to attendees and important personalities.

The highlight of this latest celebration, which was surprising to Zimen and to some Yumen, was the reciting of the planet's pledge of allegiance by Yumen from the Sunfuss Region. These Yumen, with their dusty hands on their heads, turned their backs on the Sun and, at the sound of a standing bell, jumped three steps backward shouting, "We pledge our undying love and loyalty to the progress and happiness of Yumen and the safety and supremacy of Ousia.

We vow to serve her endlessly, and we don't need the energy of the Sun, so help us, Heddy Wiseman."

Right in the middle of the independence celebration, eight thousand elite cobra fighters from Plusia led by General Natasi and dressed in their stealth suits landed in their stealth vehicles on Planet Ousia adding another thick layer of depression. The inbuilt enemy sensors in the Lous of the Zimen stationed on the terrace picked up the invasion. These sensors picked up signals from visible and invisible enemy forces, converted them into heaviness beats depending on the rank and the number of invading enemies, and registered the total beat load and lethality into the heads of the Zimen. The higher the rank and the larger the number of attackers, the higher the heaviness beat load transmitted to the Zimen.

The Cobra fighters were all armed with the SPAND (suppression, pain, neutralization, and death) rifles. These weapons could suppress the light reserves within Zimen, neutralize their firepower, and cause unbearable pain through selective organ invasions of their Dobies, leading to slow and painful death. However, the operators of the Independence Square facility pressed the button just in time to activate the rectangular disc missile-proof feature thus protecting all Yumen who were marching or standing on the circular surface of Independence Square, leaving the Zimen on the terrace to repel the attack.

The Cobra Rangers hit Zimen from all angles with their SPAND rifles, but the Zimen responded with far greater firepower. They launched thousands of the sea, land, and air weapons trace destroyers (SLAWTADs) at the Cobra fighters. In the battle's heat, Sunia stood right under the

Sun like a killing machine. He released hundreds of electric daggers and then switched over to shooting hundreds of SLAWTADs. One of the electric daggers hit General Natasi in his right eye, leaving a big hole.

Also, thousands of Natasi's fighting forces were disfigured and neutralized by Zimen. The casualty rate among the Cobra Rangers sent a shock wave through the rank and file of the Broadway operatives and on the dusty streets of Plusia's defense forces. Among the eight thousand warriors who attacked Ousia, only thirty-seven survived; that day Natasi not only lost the battle, but he lost an eye.

General Natasi flew the rest of his troops back to Plusia to plan another attack on Sunupsville. This time he planned to wipe out every single inhabitant of the town of Sunupsville to make way for the complete takeover of Ousia and to avenge the loss of his eye. One month later, General Natasi put together a legion of the fiercest warriors of Plusia and attacked again. On the eve of the battle, Natasi assembled his forces in a desert field fifteen miles north of the mountain base of Sunupsville, called the Graveyard of Annulled Purpose (GAP) to go over the battle plan. Six hours before the battle, he gave his troops the final motivational address: "Warriors of Plusia! I want you to hold out both of your hands. Every one of you has five fingers on each hand and five toes on each foot pointing forward. Don't you?" Every one of his soldiers except one shouted, "Yes, General." General Natasi responded, "And guess what? The word *fight* is spelled with five letters meaning you were born a fighter and all we did was to perfect your fighting skills. You were taught in the military academies to fight the same enemy four times if he defeats you the first time, but today I want to change that. I am saying fight your enemy as many times as possible until you defeat him. Fight him with your head, your guts, and your heart. Fight him with every ounce of your flesh to the last drop of your blood. Fight with the sole aim of resting your victorious toes on the stone heart of your enemy and closing his still eyes with the tip of your sword. In the quest to defeat your enemy, don't look back. Always look forward with optimism, faith in yourself, determination, and dedication. Comrades, this kind of fight is called total war! In those wars, I have seen warriors of other planets dig deep into their reserves of mental and physical strength but lose to their enemies; however, their enemies never forgot the fight, and the grass on those battlefields never grew again as a testament to their passion and commitment in the fight. The land you are standing on is your land, but over those mountains in a town called Sunupsville are enemies keeping you from taking what is rightfully yours. The good news is, we raised you in warrior schools that turned you into killing machines. Now you know only one word—*victory*. Are you ready to take what belongs to you? Are you ready to fight?"

"We were ready yesterday. Let's go kills those rats!" answered the lead Cobra ranger. When he finished speaking one of his soldiers walked up to him and said, "General! I have two fingers on my right hand; I lost three at the battle of Independence Square. How should I fight?"

"How many fingers do you have on your left hand?" enquired General Natasi.

"Sir! Complete! I have five."

"Warrior of Plusia, you are missing three fingers, but is your mind complete?"

"General, I have a scar on my hand, not in my mind.

My mind is stronger than the weapons that stole my three fingers. Besides, I can still squeeze a trigger with the two remaining fingers on my right hand."

"Worthy soldier of Plusia, short-faced bear of Plusia, you are one of the sharpest and strongest arrows in my quiver. You will be very useful. I will add my ten fingers to your seven fingers, and the rest of the troops will add their fingers to our fingers. Thus we will be unbeatable."

After addressing his troops, General Natasi spelled out the battle plan to them. According to the plan, the first to attack would be the green regiment, a group of rangers specialized in the precision launch of the green cartridge series. Half of these six thousand rangers were armed with the green cartridge Ultimate Sleep Dosage Seal series 8 (USDS 8), and the other half were armed with the green cartridge USDS 12. The series 8 and 12 could put its victims to very deep sleep for eight and twelve hours respectively. The Cobra Rangers used the terms 8HAP and 12HAP (eight- or twelve-hour anesthetic pills). First, the green regiment was to move in and put all Yumen and Zimen in Sunupsville to sleep. That would make it easier to capture the city without major resistance. The Green regiment would follow. This was a group of nine thousand highly trained SPAND rifle hitmen with orders to move in and shoot every Zimen with a series of SPAND bullets depending on the level of their Lous Sun intensity. When hit by these bullets, the victims' internal power source gleaned from the Sun, which was stored in the Lous of the Zimen, would be rendered inactive. To achieve maximum success, each Zimen had to be analyzed to get an exact level of Sun intensity on their Lous. This level would determine the amount of SPAND bullets capable of locking down the Lous of the targeted Zimen thus preventing them from fighting back. Any amount of miscalculation on the side of the SPAND regiment could affect the outcome of the war.

The Cobra Dome Regiment would follow the SPAND regiment. The Cobra Dome Regiment was a force of three thousand strong technicians specialized in building enemy-specific domes. The domes were shield mechanisms against incoming missiles. They formed massive blankets in the sky that prevented the Sun's rays from reaching Zimen. After the preliminary attack by the Green Regiment and the building of the domes, the Cobra infantry battalion would launch a three-wave attack on Sunupsville. Nine thousand infantry fighters would lead the first wave of attack dubbed PAD (panic and disarmament) Squad. They would aim to take out every weapon system in Sunupsville and disarm the Zimen. They were to be followed by the ZAP Squad (Zimen annihilation phase) with orders to wipe out every single Zimen. The MAT (mopping up and takeover) Squad was to conduct the last wave of attack. Their aim was to mop up every trace of the enemy in the whole of Sunupsville and take over the town.

While the planning was going on, a group of Sun-fed Zimen who were having their usual Sun-bathing exercise received intelligence of the planned battle through the microsecond red-ray transmission device in their Lous. However, they could not get details of the plan because the red-ray device could not completely break and interpret the Cobra codes—the language of the Sunupsville operation—which was intelligible only to Cobra Rangers. This group of Zimen informed the others of their intelligence and prompted them to be ready to fight. They were to power up their Lous through the Sun exercise. To prepare for the battle, they built seven bunkers on the mountains around Sunupsville and filled each with two hundred Zimen fighters under the leadership of Captain Sunia. These fighters were capable of responding with deadly force against any enemy attack. Sunia divided the Zimen into two groups: the Sunupsville Eagles and the Sunupsville Lions. He told them to wait in their bunkers for orders.

It was a cold winter afternoon, one of the coldest in the history of Ousia. The armies were like thick-blanketed clouds of darkness in battle formation, one cloud filing right behind the other. They marched across the face of the sky to cover the face of the Sun, but this time the talking drums were silent. Notwithstanding, the sun peeped through the holes in the blanket to smile at Ousia. The streets were unusually quiet; the trees held out their food for the birds, though they skipped breakfast and lunch on purpose. That day, the cock—the faithful timekeeper of Ousia—refused to crow.

Incidentally, nature herself was reeling from the effect of the preliminary attack on Yumen, which was launched exactly fifteen minutes before midday. Within that short period, the Green Regiment had launched thousands of green cartridges USDC 12, thus putting most Yumen and Zimen to sleep. After that attack—or rather overlapping it—the SPAND Regiment moved in and fired thousands of SPAND capsules on the population of Ousia. The Cobra Rangers hit the Yumen who survived the green cartridge with SPAND bullets, which targeted a specific organ in the bodies subjecting the Yumen to excruciating pain. Also, the attack neutralized the in-built enemy sensor devices, the boomerang shield mechanisms, and the microsecond red-ray transmission systems of most Zimen. While victims were groaning in powerlessness and pain, the dome technicians went to work immediately. As the second hand of the clock raced in its final lap to push the minute hand to rest on the hour hand over the midday hour, the dome was up and running. By the time the minute hand made the first jump away from midday, nine thousand PAD Squad members emerged from the top of the mountains, marched down into the center of Sunupsville, shot thousands of Broadway Lightening Missiles (BLM), and Cobra Propelled Poisoned Stingers (CPPS) on Sunupsville and other parts of Ousia. They flattened houses to the ground. Hard rocks were forced to open up their wombs as the CPPSs cut through them like scalpels. Large trees bowed down in surrender to the sheer firepower of the Cobra Rangers, and the ground beneath the standing and fallen Yumen shook and reeled like birds on the twigs of a tiny tree tossed by a violent storm. The sounds of wailing and groaning grew to a deafening pitch as the Yumen causality rate rose to the hundreds.

The sound of artillery mixed with the agonizing cries of Ousia's population created a babel of death. But an army of Zimen armed with activated boomerang shield mechanisms came out of their bunkers and behind the PAN Squad launching missiles with their SLAWTAD thus cutting off the other two ready-to-advance squads that were waiting at the back of the mountain. Sunia ordered the Sunupsville Lions—a squad of seven hundred men—to take on the PAN Squad while the Sunupsville Eagles—an army of seven hundred Zimen—provided cover for the PAN Squad as they stopped the MAT and SAP Squads from advancing into Sunupville. The Sunupsville Lions marched down the mountains behind the PAN Squad and rounded them up. The PAN Squad, now trapped in the center of the city and cut off from reinforcement, turned back to take on the Lion fighters. This group of Zimen on whose shoulders the life of Ousia rested fought with unmatched bravery, skill, speed, and lethality. The enemy was surprised.

The PAN Squad, staring defeat in the face, burst out singing Plusia's songs of war to encourage their fighters to fight on even to the point of resting their battered frames in the bosom of death. Unwilling to surrender and unafraid of death, the Cobra Rangers fought bravely. Some took cover behind buildings, rocks, and trees to dodge the missiles of the Lion fighters; others marched bravely towards the Lion fighters but fell like leaves blown by the roaring breeze of autumn. The PAN Squad fired thousands of missiles at the Sunupsville Lions, but they bounced off the boomerang shield mechanism and hit the Cobra Rangers with double force.

When the General Natasi realized the Cobra Rangers were no match for the Zimen as their weapons were killing as many of them as the weapons of the Zimen, he signaled for reinforcements from the Plusia Warfare Council. Immediately, the Plusia Warfare Council dispatched five Plusia Crow999 Interplanetary Jets and a warship, the *Red Dust Destroyer* (RDD). However, the Sunupeville Eagles, from their vantage positions, were swift to destroy the Plusia Crow999 and warship with their SLAWTAD as they were in crushing most of the MAT and SAP Squads.

"General Natasi! The other five fingers on my left hand

are gone! Sliced off by the flaming sword of a Zimen fighter," shouted the two-fingered Cobra fighter.

"Darkney warrior, my ten fingers are exhausted, and I have lost so many heads. It's time to order the troops to retreat," replied General Natasi. He gave the order for the remaining six hundred of his eleven thousand troops that were behind the mountain to retreat to the GAP Desert Field into interplanetary vehicles that were waiting to fly them back to Plusia. General Natasi had lost all nine thousand of his troops in Sunupsville to the bravery and firepower of the Zimen.

As the sound of guns and bombs died down and silence swept over Sunupsville, the cock finally crowed, the trees clapped their hands, the dark clouds raced back to their houses, and the Sun smiled incessantly. Captain Sunia and his army of fourteen hundred Zimen had defeated Plusia's army of twenty thousand warriors. Despite the loss of hundreds of Yumen, Sunupsville erupted in celebration of victory, and a new spirit of faith in the fighting skills of Zimen and quality of Ousia fighters was born.

However, Sunia and his army of Zimen stood forever tall in the hearts of Ousia but short in the temper of Plusia. In Plusia, the annual meeting for all the generals, heads of departments, regional governors, and captains of special forces was held on the last day of every calendar year, just before the dawn of a new year. At these meetings, leaders presented their reports, strategies were revised, new plans were rolled out, challenges were deliberated, and new assignments were given. In the Year of the Lion, leading to the Year of the Dragon, which was the sixth-year rule of King Heddy Wiseman, who was the seventh king of planet

Ousia, an all-important meeting took place at the military headquarters in Plusia chaired by King Plavar. The theme was "Strategic Weapons in the Taking Over of Ousia." At this meeting, chairman of the military council, General Natasi, gave a briefing. Before he could utter any word, he pointed his bony finger to the motto of the Total Enemy Plusialisation Plan, the act of taking over Ousia and make it Plusia. This was written on the ceiling of the amphitheater, and it read "Destroy Disappear, and Dominate."

With every head lifted and all eyes focused on the motto, he said, "Comrades, this motto has been our eyes and hearts for centuries. Today let us take this commitment a notch higher. Let it become the very blood that flows through our veins." The one-eyed general pointed to the empty socket on his face, which he referred to his medal of valor and necessary sacrifice to the greatest cause in the history of Plusia's military council: the destruction and enslavement of all Yumen. "See this hole in my face?" bellowed General Natasi. "I lost my eye to Sunia in the Battle of Independence Square. This hole in my face serves as my reminder to take over Planet Ousia. The name Sunia stinks to the highest heavens. I hate that name and will never rest until I kill that goat and use his head as a dish to serve wine to the gods!" screamed Natasi. Blinded by his hatred for Yumen, General Natasi claimed he lost one eye so he could have just one eye entirely focused on crushing Zimen, especially Sunia. When he looked at the rearview mirror of war, he saw defeat, but his desperate desire for victory and his hatred for Yumen were sure to fuel more wars. Asking his audience to look at the Broadway motto and his eyeless socket was a very unusual way for the head of the warfare council to start his talk, even though it helped heighten the venom for Yumen in the hearts of his audience. However, the point he was making to a hall full of very accomplished and elite military generals was that the enduring power of a successful mission rested not on honors engraved on pieces of metal and worn on their chests and shoulders as testaments of their present rank and past sacrifices; rather, it rested on another kind of medal—the living medals worn by dead warriors. As a well-decorated soldier himself, he sought to turn the attention of his audience to the spirit and courage of dead and dismembered fighters of Plusia. He wanted to remind them of the urgency of their cause, the lifetime nature of their sacrifice, and the honor of the ultimate price of death for the successful takeover of Ousia. "Comrades of the armed forces of Plusia, fighters of the greatest military in the history of Plusia, today I take these gold medals off my shoulder and chest and hang them on my spine. I want to hide those reminders of blinding glory from friends and foes alike. From now onward, this is my glory!" said General Natasi pointing to his eyeless socket. "I want to dedicate this medal to those who died on the battlefields in their attempt to take over Ousia!" he screamed pounding the surface of the lectern. "Inside the mountains and hills of Ousia, very deep in her cold womb, are our fallen warriors. In the heart of her hills are your lost fingers, your hands, your heads, your bodies, and my eye. Comrades, buried deep in those mountains of dirt are your fears, your failures, and your foes. Let us make Planet Ousia Yumenless and Zimenless! This is our planet! This is our home!"

The entire hall erupted with a marathon of applause. When the applause finally died down, Natasi said, "Well, folks, that is just an introduction. Let us get into the meat and bones of tonight's briefing." Natasi told the audience about the work his forces were doing and their great accomplishments and failures. "Our Broadway operatives have done very well. Ninety percent of Yumen are now under my control, except for the ten percent still occupied by Zimen. Every single Yumen disarmed by our Broadway operatives or through their many agents or affected Yumen under stage one—called the wedge threshold barometer, which is to turn every Yumen against the Sun and Zimen— is part of a grand plan called Total Enemy Plusialisation. This is the plan to either take the minds or the lives of Yumen. As you all know, the minds of Yumen are their most powerful weapons, and they are what activate all other weapons. Therefore, if we cannot take their minds, we take their lives. Simple! One of the most successful tools in taking the minds of Yumen has been our custom-made Plesordol drug, which has worked wonders in cutting the link between their heads and their chests and made their Lous defective. Once they have surrendered their minds, we put them under the broad lenses of the Cobra Forces to monitor and maintain a lifestyle of defeat. They live in a state of operational inactiveness in an atmosphere of suppression. We have been able to achieve this by hiding our identity, mixing with Yumen, and flooding the Ousia market with large quantities of Plesordol. The second stage of the Total Enemy Plusialisation Plan is the complete takeover of Ousia. This involves killing every Yumen unaffected by the Plusia infiltration process, enslaving affected Yumen, and moving every Darkney from planet Plusia to Ousia. However, for this to happen, we need to conquer the remaining ten percent of the territory still in the hands of Zimen. We fought against them in the Battle of Independence Square and the Battle of Sunupsville and lost both battles. However, Plusia shall not sleep till vengeance, like a tsunami, rolls over Ousia and Sunia, drowning them into the depth of the dark sea of Plusia's anger. Comrades! Let's keep fighting. We have sown division in Ousia through cranial warfare. The dusty dance of Plusia has left Yumen powerless. We are controlling the impulses of most Yumen and have transformed them into active agents and sometimes passive allies in our fight against Zimen. Let's keep fighting! Let's be focused! We are winning the war! I thank you all."

At the end of his talk, General Natasi saluted his comrades, and they responded with a loud shout of, "Auzzza! Buzzzza! Cuzzza! Duzzza!" This was the usual response of honor to respected warriors of Plusia.

CHAPTER 5

The Systematic Takeover of Ousia

These dark-hearted warriors from Plusia quickly disarmed mountains of resistance through skin love; fake smiles; and long, dusty handshakes.

Thereafter, King Plavar of Plusia stood up to roll out his new strategy and to give his closing remarks. He informed the assembly of the council's decision to, in the short term, suspend all large-scale conventional attacks and focus instead on guerilla warfare alongside the ongoing cranial warfare, dance warfare, and impulse warfare. He said they would ambush and destroy Zimen in the Sunbond Region one at a time using a custom-made weapons that would penetrate the boomerang shield mechanism. They would go ahead with their plans to move all Darkneys from Plusia to the colder and darker regions of Ousia: the Sunshun Region and the Sunfuss Region.

According to this plan, they would arrive in batches pretending to be tourists from another planet. Slowly, they would worm their way into leadership positions with the power to influence decisions that would systematically transform Ousia into Plusia. After the takeover, they would proceed with the ambitious plan of developing the Sunshun and Sunfuss Regions of Ousia to the crowning glory of Ousia to lure Zimen away from Sunbond to Sunfuss and Sunshun territories and kill them in Sunlesville the capital city of the Sunfuss Region followed by a takeover war on the streets of Sunupsville. They would make these regions so attractive that, instead of gazing at the Sun, Zimen would come from the Sunbond Region to gaze at the wonders of Sunfuss and Sunshun Regions thus causing the Zimen to lose their Sun power and render their weapon systems inactive.

After reducing the population of Zimen through the Sunfuss and Sunshun ambush strategies, Darkneys would attack the remaining Zimen in the Sunbond Region with a customized weapon system. Therefore, King Plavar gave the assignment to General Jupiter, the head of the Jupiter Squadron, to develop a customized weapon to destroy Zimen. In closing, King Plavar said to his warriors, "Tonight when general Natasi spoke, he stood on the Yumen symbolic portrait on the stage of this building. When you walked into this building, you each marched on that symbolic portrait at the entrance of this building. So now with your drawn-out swords, let's form a circle around this faded portrait on the stage. Let us cover every ounce of the portrait with the tips of our swords as we once again reaffirm our undying commitment to pursuing our single aim: the destruction of all Yumen."

The cooperate reaffirmation of hatred and unity of a

purpose to destroy the enemy ended the briefing. After the briefing, all the warriors went back to their stations of assignment. Later that night, a group of one hundred Darkneys disguised as tourists landed in the Sunshun Region. They wore big smiles on their dusty faces, which Yumen mistook for facial cosmetics. They were quick to extend a handshake to every Yumen, and their kindness, like a sledgehammer, knocked down every wall of suspicion. Their soft words like morning dew washed away the dust of hesitation from Yumen and transform withered leaves of hate to buoyant oaks of trust which, like a lubricant, helped worm their way into the cold hearts of Yumen. These dark-hearted warriors from Plusia quickly disarmed mountains of resistance through skin love, fake smiles, and long dusty handshakes. More so, what further cemented their unity was their common hatred for the Sun and a love affair with cold temperatures. Shortly, Yumen began to welcome them into their homes, gave them lands, and begged them to stay. At the request of Yumen, more and more Darkneys landed in the Sunshun and Sunfuss Regions and made these areas their home.

Unbeknownst to Yumen, moving all Darkneys from Plusia to Ousia under the grand takeover plan had begun. They worked in strategic institutions and rose to leadership positions, thus altering the direction and chemistry of the Sunshun and Sunfuss Regions. By force of number and strength of vision, the Plusia culture became the dominant culture in the two regions, so much so that it was very difficult to tell the difference between Darkneys and Yumen living in the Sunshun and Sunfuss Regions.

So indelible was the impact of Plusia's culture on

Yumen that king Plavar of Plusia—the master builder and visionary—was crowned king of the united Sunfuss and Sunshun Regions. In the first year of his reign, he rolled out plans to build massive road infrastructures linking both regions, and he transformed the skyline of Ousia with buildings that looked like a constellation of very tall stars. Also, he was a very able diplomat who united Yumen and Darkneys under the name Dartmen, causing all opposing identities and allegiances to evaporate. He brought the Carnival of the Dusty Dance to the united regions, which served as a social cement between Yumen and Darkneys.

In the Sunfuss Region, the Carnival of the Dusty Dance lasted for a month. The climax of the event was held on last day of the month in an open field at Sunlesville, capital of the Sunfuss Region. On that day, citizens of the united region, including the king, gathered at Sunlesville to dance the dusty dance. Early that morning, Yumen who were determined to get rid of the golden hats searched for them in every nook and cranny of their houses and strew them on the ground in the open field. It was a special dance to most Darkneys because they danced on foreign soil littered with golden hats. That day, all the united regions turned their backs on the Sunbond Region and stomped their feet continually on the dusty field full of golden hats so hard that the whole of Ousia shook, sending tremors to the mountains of Sunupsville. When the dance was over, tiny shredded pieces of the golden hats were scattered on the ground; the dusty feet of the Dartmen had shredded the golden hats and made dirty the tiny pieces. After the all-important dance, Darkneys rejoiced at the progress of their plans as the wind blew away the tiny pieces of the golden hats in a different directions across the Sunfuss Region.

Next, King Plavar and his military council turned their attention to reducing the number of Zimen in the Sunbond Region by ambushing them on Lukewarm Boulevard, the road linking the united region to the Sunbond Region. Lukewarm Boulevard was a single-lane road sandwiched between the sea on one side and trees planted on the opposite shoulder of the road. The green lush foliage formed a canopy against the heat of the Sun. The cool breeze from the sea and the shade from the trees combined with the scenery of scattered mountains and little hills provided a great appeal to travelers and fuel for the journey. Many travelers lay their weary backs on the trunks of the trees on Lukewarm Boulevard and slept under the cool air-conditioning provided by nature. This innocent-looking road became the new front in a dastardly battle waged on Zimen. The eleven Broadway Street operatives who had moved to the Sunfuss Region, led by General Deesix, were stationed along the road. Some wrapped themselves in leaves as a camouflage, climbed up into the trees, and hid in its branches; others hid under the water awaiting signals from the warriors in the trees to attack. They waited until the weary traveling Zimen were fast asleep under the trees. They then struck them with the deadly Jupitech Zee missiles, missiles custom-made by Jupiter squadron to penetrate the boomerang shield mechanisms of Zimen. The warriors then whisked the Zimen's Dobies away to be burnt.

The Jupitech Zee missiles proved to very effective in killing, especially sleeping Zimen on Lukewarm Boulevard. For that reason, the Dartmen were eager to try it on

Sun-charged Zimen in Sunupsville. A few Zimen made it to the united region, but they never made it back to the Sunbond Region because Dartmen hunted and killed them on the streets on Sunlesville. Hundreds of Zimen were warned not to make the journey, but unheeding the warning, they were ambushed and killed on Lukewarm Boulevard. This caused the unhappy and disappointed Sunia to lament thus: "Oh, Lukewarm Boulevard, the graveyard of the Sun's warriors, beyond your embracing leaves of love and gentle waves singing like a nightingale lies the sting of death. You have killed more Zimen than all the wars of Ousia combined! Oh, Lukewarm Boulevard, you have forced more tears from the Sun than the sea that caresses your tiny banks, yet the Sun and his sons shall win this war. We are fighters! We are Zimen!" While Sunia and most of the citizens of Sunupsville lamented the fate of the fallen Zimen, King Plavar and his council of elders were celebrating their military success.

CHAPTER 6

Zimen Defend Sunuspville

We did not ask for this war, but it reaffirms our very essence as Zimen, and its outcome will forever stand as a testament to all generations that the Sun-powered Yumen— Zimen—fight like no one else.

With all the Zimen causalities, Sunia knew it was a matter of time before the enemy took the battle from Lukewarm Boulevard to the streets of Sunupsville. Therefore, he rallied the remaining Zimen of the Sunbond Region and summoned them to a meeting in an old tunnel deep under the mountains of Sunupsville a few miles away from the road linking the Sunbond Region and the united regions. About one hundred feet in front of the assembled Zimen was a makeshift lectern made from the stump of a dead birch tree. There was an old firepit to the immediate right of the lectern; it was still burning strong and discharging heat into the tunnel.

Sunia stood behind the lectern to talk. He looked at

the raging fire for a while without uttering a word as sparks flew upward and ashes fall. The intensity of his gaze and the reflection of the burning fire in his eyes reflected the moment. It was a moment for harnessing the fires in Zimen to defend Sunupsville. Finally, he turned his gaze to his fellow Zimen, broke his silence, and said to them, "I hear a distant sound of war. It's a loud sound, a furious sound, a terminus sound. The warriors of darkness are matching toward Sunupsville; their march is hasty, it's noisy, and it's deadly. Their cold steps are fueled by the ashes of Zimen who fell on Lukewarm Boulevard. This is the march of a vast hate against Sunupsville and it is led by a decorated warrior by the name of General Deenine who also happens to be Natasi. The drum majors of Plusia are beating the drums of war."

Then Sunia paused for a deep breath, placed his index finger on his chin, looked intensely at the faces of the audience, and muttered these words: "There are few moments in life when the brush of history paints the portraits of heroes or blacks out the names of cowards. The footsteps of such moments are at the door of Sunupsville. Our forebears told us the Sun is a canvas of faces—the faces of Zimen who fight on the side of order. The occasion to paint your face on the highest and unfaded canvas of Ousia to reflect on the faces of young and old is fast approaching. Will you paint your faces?"

Together, every single Zimen in the audience screamed, "Yezzzzzzz! We will paint our faces on the Sun!" Thereafter, one Zimen in the crowd shouted, "I will paint my face gold!" Another said, "I like blue—a blue reflection on Ousia is a good thing! I will paint mine blue."

"We are fighters!" screamed Sunia at the very top of his voice. "And this is the moment of purpose! However, we need the power to drive purpose, so let's put more hours into the Sun-concentration exercise. When our purpose unites with power, there is nothing we cannot conquer. Then Sunia told the Zimen to draw near and form a big circle around the raging fire so that together they could unite their threads of passion and weave it into a fabric of courage. As they placed their right hands across their chests, he ordered them to bind their collective courage—steel courage made in the crucibles of war—with an oath of allegiance. Sunia reminded them they belonged to a long tradition of fearless fighters who had given their bodies to the fires of war in the defense of Ousia.

After the oath of allegiance to fight together till every ounce of their Dobies and sparks on their Lous had gone, the Zimen walked among each other, giving each other triple pats on the shoulder along with warm embraces. And with unblinking eye contact, they all shook hands vigorously. Before they departed to their houses, all the Zimen agreed to prepare for war. They also agreed to meet again the following day to start the work of extending and modernizing the tunnels through the mountains with access to strategic locations on top of the mountains. Also, they agreed to put extra hours into the Sun-concentration exercises to charge the batteries of their weapons systems and store up extra power that would last them throughout their time in the tunnel and beyond.

The work of repairing and extending the old tunnels started at midday the following day. That day, the Sun wore a very warm smile and dispensed great heat to make the Zimen invisible to Dartmen as thousands of Zimen worked tirelessly to repair and modernized the tunnel to withstand missile strikes and to fit the battle plan. They linked the isolated tunnels to form a horizontal track that held two horses. The improved system had strategic disguised vertical tubes to certain parts of the mountain and through it.

After building the tunnels, Sunia chose thirty-seven of the most brilliant Zimen to design three models of the most lethal external weapons of war and produce forty units each of each model. These Zimen came up with the Ouvic777, an oval-shaped stealth air vehicle armed with a ninety-nine nuclear laser rifles positioned around it with the capability to melt or cause to malfunction anything its laser touched. Each of its rifles had a 180-degree rotational capability. The massive disk that glided through the sky silently took off at the speed of light and moved in any direction without having to turn. Also, the Zimen designed and built the Roboyum, a remote-controlled robotic Yumen with two high-definition cameras as eyes through which the operators could monitor their targets. Also, both hands of a Roboyum were missile launchers. Each Roboyum carried a backpack of ten missiles the shape and size of a basketball, each loaded with lethal explosives that could wipe out any object in the perimeter of a soccer field. Similarly, they made the Macaquavic333, a stealth aquatic missile launcher in the shape of a boat. It had three separate cannons, and each barrel had three missile vents. At the press of a button, it released nine jumbo missiles, each the size of a minivan capable of causing untold destruction.

As Sunia and his army of Zimen were preparing to defend Sunupsville against any act of aggression, the Plusia military councils of the united region were putting finishing touches to their plans to take over Sunupsville. The victories over Zimen on Lukewarm Boulevard motivated the military council of Plusia to make the Sunbond Region an irresistible takeover target. Knowing they could not fight well in the heat and light of the Sunbond Region, they constantly monitored the weather conditions, intending to strike when dark clouds covered the Sun and when the temperature fell below zero degrees. However, the faithfulness and dedication of the Sun to maintain a broad and sizzling smile every day disappointed them. The Broadway Military Council, after consultation with the national chief shaman, decided on the technique of artificial Sun hooding through the dusty dance of Plusia. According to the chief shaman, the Sun would put on its black hood when they directed a large number of dust particles into its eyes. Through this technique, the Military Council could control the timeframe for the takeover of the Sunbond Region.

In this vein, they announced a one-month-long festival of the dusty dance, compelling all Dartmen within the Sunfuss and Sunshun Regions to take part in the festival. Like an army of driver ants in search of food, Dartmen from both regions swarmed the dusty fields of Sunlessville. They danced so hard and so long they sent tremors into the living rooms of Sunupsville. As the Darkneys danced on dusty fields across the two regions, many dust particles made their way to the Sunbond Region, covering the sky, painting it brown. As the dance continued, the dust in the sky formed an image of an octopus with very long tentacles. The tentacles wrapped around the face of the Sun, thus closing its eyes. Throughout the history of Ousia, there had been only two occasions when the Sun closed its eyes. The first time was when the Darkneys introduced the dusty dance of Plusia to Yumen in Ousia; the second time was when many enemies invaded Ousia filling the sky with their smoky war vehicles.

As darkness fell over the Sunbond Region, the Zimen interpreted the sudden greyness as a sign of impending enemy invasion. This was confirmed by intelligence of enemy attack. Quickly, they went into battle mode. Sunia ordered every Zimen in Sunupsville into the tunnels. He then ordered the deployment of remote-controlled Roboyum in all the streets of Sununpsville. Also, he ordered the deployment of the Macaquavic333 to patrol the seas and got the Ouvic777 ready for action to protect the airspace of the Sunbond Region.

The Military Council of the United Region predicted that a one-month-long mega dusty dance would veil the Sun for at least a week—the length of time they planned for their military operation. On the last day of the festival, thousands of Cobra Rangers rolled down on Sunupsville and captured the mountains of Sunupsville with no resistance from Zimen. The Marine Defense Forces under the command of General Synke were far out at sea waiting for the command to launch their missiles on Sunupville. Similarly, the Jupiter Squadron armed with their Crow999 Interplanetary Jets stationed at the Sunfuss Region airfield four hundred and ninety kilometers outside Sunupsville waited for the command to strike their targets. The Zimen could see every single enemy movement through the eyes of the Roboyum and the Ouvic777 which projected live images on a screen inside the tunnels. The Zimen began a sustained missile bombardment of Dartmen on the mountain through the Roboyum, killing many of them. The Cobra Rangers, under the leadership of General Natasi, mistook the Roboyum for real Zimen and responded with far greater firepower; missiles were falling on Sunupsville from all around the surrounding mountains like rain on a desert land, destroying most of the Roboyum. The Zimen held their fire and moved the remaining twenty-one Roboyum to strategic locations to provide a vision of the movement of the enemy.

After six hours of intense, non-stop artillery engagement from both sides, there was an eerie silence all over Sunupsville that convinced General Natasi they had neutralized major threats. He ordered a large number of his forces expert in hand-to-hand combat to advance to the heart of Sunupville to take every inch while some Cobra Rangers held down the mountains.

As soon as Natasi's fighters got to the heart of the city, Sunia ordered the Ouvic777 to obliterate all the forces on the mountains and the Macaquavic333 to sail far out into the sea and destroy all enemy warships. The forty Ouvic777s took off, covered the airspace of Sunupsville, and rained down its nuclear lasers on the forces on the mountain, destroying every one of them.

General Natasi radioed General Jupiter, commander of the Plusia Air Force, and asked Jupiter Squadron to provide air cover and reinforcement. But the Ouvic777s had shot down every single Plusia Crow999 in the airspace of the Sunbond Region. They had then flown over the Sunfuss airfield and destroyed all the Plusia air vehicles.

Thereafter, Sunia ordered all the Zimen out of the tunnels to engage the Cobra Rangers on the streets of Sunuspville, but they were outnumbered by the Cobra fighters. The protracted battle without the Sun's energy weakened some Zimen, and they fell in their hundreds under the energetic Cobra fighters armed with the Jupiter Zee Missile Launchers.

Then, suddenly, a gentle wind blew across the skies of Sunbond Region, pushing back the tentacles of the dust cloud. The dust moved away from the Sun. The smiling Sun beamed its strongest-ever heat and light on Sunupsville, blinding and weakening the Cobra fighters but invigorating the Zimen. Quickly, the tide of war tilted in favor of the Zimen; the Cobra forces within Sunupsville, including General Deesix and the few fighters who had run up into the mountains, were destroyed by the Ouvic777s.

Sunia hit General Natasi on his chest with an electric sword. The general groaned aloud in pain, dropped to his knees, and whispered silently to himself, "I have been hit by a sword from the heart of a Zimen—the elite of them all. Our fears are like winged birds. They fly swiftly ahead of us and wait patiently to sink their cold claws into our hearts."

As Sunia walked toward General Natasi, the general declared, "Sunia, your sword has cut down the tree that provides shades to Plusia."

When Sunia reached Natasi, he kicked him on his stomach very hard; General Natasi fell on his side and then Sunia put his right foot on his neck and said, "General Natasi! You are the architect of Ousia's troubles. Since the day you infiltrated my planet, I have dreamed of planting my sword deep into your chest and killing you myself."

"Sunia," grunted General Natasi, "a Darkney warrior does not die. His spirit lives on and takes residence in the body of living Darkneys. Your sword might force me to leave my body before its time, but, Sunia, we will meet again, and at that time, you will have to contend with two Natasis in one body."

"Natasi, my resolve to defeat evil and preserve order is unshakable, and my dedication to effect conquest is matchless. If a thousand Natasis were to rise from your dying breath, I would defeat them again and again."

General Natasi replied, "Worthy soldier of Ousia, you might have defeated the short-faced bears of Plusia, but there is one more enemy to contend with—the ferocious monster within each Yumen that feeds from my Plesordol and the Friskey-Six wine, making Yumen headless and blind. Will you be able to defeat those monsters?"

"Deenine, my orders are to kill you and defeat your forces. However, all Yumen have the responsibility to face their monsters and defeat them. For some, it will mean depriving the monster of the food it loves and starving it to death. For others it will mean looking at the Sun intensively a little longer," replied Sunia. "Take my hand, brave son of Ousia!" Natasi tried to lift his right hand but dropped it again and breathed his last. "Natasi is dead! The evil General Natasi is no more! Zimen we have won the battle!" screamed Sunia.

After the victory, Sunia and his host of Zimen marched across town on the rubble of Sunupville. Some celebrated a great victory while others mourned the ruins of the city. As they marched across the city, they stopped to look at the ruin of the building that had once housed the Museum of War History. Amid twisted metal and ashes, Sunia saw a badly burned book lying under a heap of dirt. Wondering what written record of Ousia's history had survived the war, he picked up the book and flipped through the layers of its crumpled pages. When he got to the last page, which was still intact, he noticed an ancient prophecy. Silently, Sunia read its sacred lines. Each line pushed his eyelids back until his eyes were wide open. When he finished, his jaw dropped in wonder at the timeliness and resonance of its message. "Hey, comrades, you must hear these words," exclaimed Sunia. He ordered his fighting forces to listen up as he read aloud the words to them. "There are no befitting words for this moment in history like these immortal words enshrined in the surviving page of a book containing the words of an unknown seer," said Sunia as he wiped the sweat off his brow with his ash-stained hand, leaving four horizontal grey lines on his forehead. He paused and glanced as far as his eyes could see at the vast ruin of Sunupsville and said, "sons of the Sun, listen to the living words of prophecy from these limp pages: 'Behold they will come from afar, dark warriors flying on the wings of hate turning the heart of the sons of Ousia against the Sun. They will march on the golden hats of Ousia. Their dusty feet shall turn Ousia dark. The weapons of war shall thunder on Ousia dividing her into three worlds. Ousia shall dance and drop like leaves in the way of a storm in the fall, but the sons of the Sun shall arise with healing and victory in their Lous. They will clasp their hands into the hand of her angry son, and the enemies like wax shall melt. Then one war shall lead to another until the first is content to be the last.'"

After Sunia finished reading the prophecy, Zimen were elated, not because of the promise of peace, but because they had been described as the fighting machines of history and channels of peace as foretold thousands of years ago. Sunia put both of his hands on his chest, looked at the top of the mountains, and said to his fellow Zimen, "Listen! Did you hear that? I hear victory songs rolling down the mountains. Unlock your Lous and get ready to shoot!"

All the Zimen turned around pointed their weapons in the direction of the noise, but they saw thousands of Yumen with palm branches in their hands singing a song of triumph as they marched down the mountain toward them. "Put all your weapons back in their chambers!" ordered Sunia.

As the group got closer, Sunia noticed that Soggy was leading the group. All the Zimen joined in singing the songs of triumph; four of the most respected Zimen rushed toward Sunia and lifted him onto their shoulders, but Sunia bade them put him down. When his feet touched the ground, Soggy ran toward him, fell on his knees and said, "Great defender of Ousia! son of the Sun! I have come late—very late—but I have come to Sunupsville. I walked on the crooked path of my frustrations through blinding curves of hopelessness and climbed the mountains of my failures to this hallowed ground of victory. We have come to Sunupsville! All these Yumen standing behind me have come. Every one of us has fought a bitter battle with Friskey-Six and Plesordol on the many corners of Broadway Street and have won. Now we can see the Sun clearly, and our heads are functioning well."

"Welcome, Soggy. Welcome every one of you to Sunupsville. It is never too late to start all over again. Moreover, you give me hope that the monster within Yumen can be defeated and that shadows can have limited lifespans." Then Sunia looked at his fellow Zimen and said to them, "This victory belongs to you! As sweet as this victory is, let us not forget that the war is not over. Zimen, we have entered a new chapter in the history of warfare on planet Ousia. The Battle of Sunupsville has brought to the fore new and painful realities that will require a new level of sleepless vigilance by all Zimen. The old rules of engagement must change to include three realities: Some Yumen—our brothers, the fighting machines of Ousia—are fighting on the side of the enemy; Darkneys—our enemies and masters of the Stealth Jacket Technology—are now living on our planet; most Yumen amongst us have swung wide open the door to enemy attacks. Notwithstanding, we never surrendered, and we *will* never surrender to the enemy. No! Never! We would rather die than surrender! However, if we die, say, at age seventy, when the elders of Ousia come to eulogize us, let them tell Ousians we lived four-hundred-and-ninety years (multiply seventy by a phantom seven). The million vibrations from Darkneys like sharp tiny daggers on our frames that sent every cell of our bodies reluctantly marching forward at lightning speed, let them multiply it! The effect of heaviness beat projected at our Dobies through countless enemy invasions, all of this makes up the phantom seven. Multiply it! Let future generations multiply it! Two cold hateful eyes the size of tennis balls multiplied by millions looking at us projecting a banquet of pain on our frame. Multiply it! Multiply it by the unseen number. Ours was an endless night. The agonizing weight of wasted Yumen on the battlefield of Ousia troubled us consistently. The years of war meant to destroy Zimen have made us granite tough and helped focus our attention on what is important: our purpose. It has helped us to harness the Sun's energy to actualize it. Henceforth, our eyes will avoid the distractions of Ousia and focus more on the heat and glow of the Sun."

Sunia paused for a minute or two, looked at the mountains around Sunupsville, and pointed his thick finger to the mountain range and shouted, "Hey, Zimen, lift your scarlet eyes and look at the mountains strewn with the remains of your enemies. We did not ask for this war, but it reaffirms our very essence as Zimen, and its outcome will forever stand as a testament to all generations that the Sun-powered Yumen—Zimen—fight like no one else."

Then one Zimen from the crowd lifted his right hand in the air, jumped up, and shouted, "Sunia! Sunia! I want to speak!"

"Speak, comrade, speak!" answered Sunia.

"Wars are ugly, yet fighting wars is the oxygen of our lives. We live when we fight a good fight; we die when we surrender to evil and disorder."

Sunia shook his head in affirmation and said to the crowd of Zimen, "Those words sum up the spirit and story of Zimen. Ousia is proud of you! This story, like the story of the bravery of our forebears, will forever be etched on the hearts and minds of future generations. Arise, sons of the Sun! Let's put our power and purpose into use once more by starting the work of rebuilding Sunupsville into a city that will serve as a mirror of purpose, beauty, and order for the whole of Ousia and other planets."

Printed in the United States
By Bookmasters